I0612354

Master Minds

A

T.S. Connor Novel

A T.S. Connor Book

Published by T.S. Connor Publishing INC.

Copyright © 2018 Taniqua Connor

All rights reserved. No part of this book may be reproduced or transmitted in any form or by any means, electronic or mechanical, including photocopying, recording, or by any information storage and retrieval system, without the written permission of the publisher, except where permitted by law. For more information please contact T.S. Connor at AuthorTSConnor.com

ISBN: 978-1-5136-4398-4

Acknowledgements

First and foremost, I'd like to thank the Most High for blessing me with a vivid imagination and the ability to have a unique way with words. I'd like to thank everyone who has supported my career as a writer thus far, as always, it's much appreciated. Shout out to the gentlemen Damone Powell and Alexander McElvain who let me interview them for research on the male's psyche. Shout out to my graphic designer who always brings my visions to life, Derek Jones. Shout out to the models on the cover who played their roles perfectly, Terry Junior and Nicholas Bryant. Thank you to my aunt Alexis and my sister Quaniqua for being my critics. Special thanks to my editor who always help me perfect my craft, Valerie D. Most importantly, thank you to my mother and my daughter for always being my rock!

Also by T.S. Connor

He's Mine: A Romance Novel

To those ambitious souls who believe in no

limitations, this is for you.

Chapter One:

Then

"I'm hungry. Man, we ain't got nothing to eat in this raggedy house. Tony, what we gone do?" asked Byron as he held his growling stomach.

"Don't worry B, I'll handle it. I'll find us something to eat." I announced as I searched the kitchen cabinets for an inkling of food. We were going on day two with no food and my parents were in a slumber from being drunk and high.

It's funny how I was taking care of my brothers at thirteen years old as if I was a grown ass man. Byron, Jasper, Julian and Tevin weren't my blood brothers but blood couldn't make us any closer. We all grew up in foster care together and as the oldest I felt obligated to make sure my brothers were taken care of. We coined ourselves as "brothers from unknown mothers". We been bonding since we were adopted by these so called "foster parents" who happened to be a married, middle-aged white couple. If you ask me, the only reason they adopted five black boys was to collect a check from the state. It's clear what they did with the money because they damn sure weren't providing a healthy environment for my brothers and me.

"Why can't we just run in the corner store and grab some shit like we did yesterday? I swear I'm about to die from starvation!" yelled Byron. I loved Byron but this nigga was a hot head. I always told him, "Whatever you put out into the world is what you're going to attract back." Unlike me, this nigga just didn't understand how the universe works.

"No, we're not going back to the corner store. I don't want that bad karma on my hands. Just trust me!" I finally found some expired crackers on top of the refrigerator. It wasn't much but it was something that could fill us up until I could think of something else.

We all circled in the middle of the living room floor. I watched them devour those crackers like it was steak and potatoes. It was at that very moment when I made the declaration that this would be the last time I let any of us suffer. I sat in silence and tried to think of a way to generate some money in order to buy us some food. I may not have had any money at the moment but one thing I did have was a high intellect and it was time to put it to use.

"Stay here. I'll be right back," I announced as I stood up and dusted off my old jeans full of holes. I went to my room and grabbed my chess board.

"Where you going bro?" asked Jasper as he licked his fingers.

"I'm going to the park. I got a plan to hustle up some money the legit way."

"Well if you going, I'm going too. We all could probably come up," said Tevin.

"Alright, hurry up and get dressed."

As I opened the front door, I noticed two older black women who were just about to knock. There were bags and boxes on our front porch as they looked down and smiled at us.

"Is the man of the house around?" asked one of the older women.

"I guess you can say I'm the man of the house. Can I help you?" I asked as I stepped onto the porch.

"Just the little man I wanted to see. I'm a member of the church that's just a few blocks away and we're going door to door giving away food and books. I've seen you little boys around and I just wanted to give you a few things."

"Thanks for thinking of us. I'll take these," I said as I bent down and picked up the boxes full of books.

Jasper and Tevin grabbed some of the bags that were on the porch and headed back inside the house. As I grabbed the last bag I could see its contents. This bag didn't contain your typical cheap food and non-perishable canned goods; everything was organic and natural. Even the chicken and steak were made from grass-fed, cage-free animals. I know churches aren't in the business of giving away food that cost an arm and a leg so I wondered, "Who really had a hand in giving us this food?" I was grateful nonetheless and silently thanked whoever sent this to us because I was starving. However, my curiosity still got the best of me.

"I just want to thank you ladies again but I'm also curious. I'm sure this food is really expensive so may I ask who sent this over?" Both ladies looked at each other and smiled once again.

"You are one smart little man. Let's just say you have some guardian angels watching over you. We'll be around to check on you and your brothers frequently. Be safe out here." The ladies hugged me and headed towards the sidewalk.

I took the rest of the food inside and rushed to the living room window. Pushing back the sheets that served as curtains, I watched them leave until they were out of my line of sight. I noticed that they didn't stop at any other house which made me wonder if they really were going "door to door" like they had previously mentioned. After putting up the food, we headed to the park to hustle up some money. Just because we were lucky enough to now have some food didn't mean it would happen again.

It was packed when we made it to the park. The basketball court was full of brothers running pickup games, kids were on the playground swings, and there was a rapid chess tournament already in full swing. In our neck of the woods chess was more than just a game. It was a test of your mental capabilities. Could you strategize efficiently and swiftly all while killing your opponent? If you were anything like me, then you would love a mind sport such as this one and all the bragging rights that came along with it.

I sat on the sidelines and watched a game between these two older black dudes. The game was intense because both men knew the game well and knew how to strategically move their pieces. I'd seen these dudes around before. Each of them had earned mad respect in the neighborhood. One of them was known as Von. He was an older cat with a few successful businesses under his belt and a lot of money in his pocket. If I could beat him in a game of chess, then I'm sure I could gain his respect and his connections. Von ended up winning that game so I took a seat across from him thinking, "This was my chance!" He was draped in gold jewelry from his earlobes to the expensive watch wrapped around his wrist. He looked at me with a skeptical expression across his face as if I wouldn't even be a challenge. He just didn't know that he was dealing with an expert.

"You taking a seat lil' man like you know what you doing with this game," said Von.

"Just set up the board and play." I wasn't in the mood for trash talking. I was on a mission to beat him.

"Don't expect me to go easy on you either. You can take this ass whooping just like everybody else."

"The first move is on you. Ladies first," I said as I waited for him to make his move. I noticed the smirk on his face as he moved one of his pawns.

"What's so funny?" I asked as I moved one of my pawns as well.

"You remind me of myself when I was your age. I can tell you're smart… and cocky."

"I'm not cocky. I'm confident. There's a huge difference between the two."

"How old are you lil' man?" he asked as he moved his knight.

"I'll be fourteen in a few months. However, age doesn't define maturity or intelligence," I said as I moved my pawn and captured his knight. I could tell I impressed him.

"That's true. Some people are born with old souls and wise minds."

After capturing his knight, he decided to pay more attention to the game rather than our conversation. However, he still was no match for me. Although he was able to capture a few of my pawns, I never left my King or Queen unprotected. Anyone that knows the game knows that the queen is the most powerful piece on the board but if the king is ever captured then your opponent wins. When Von moved his knight he made the mistake of leaving his king unprotected which I happened to notice and quickly captured with my pawn. I had even impressed myself.

"Never judge a book by its cover. You never know what you're going to read," I boasted.

"Who you here with?" asked Von.

"I'm here with my little brothers. They over there on the court running a five-on-five game," I said as I pointed in the direction of the basketball court.

"What's your name lil' man?"

"My name is Antonio but everyone calls me Tony."

"You look like you can use an opportunity and I can definitely use some help down at my restaurant. Meet me at the *Sub Joint* tomorrow at 4:30 p.m. Bring your brothers too and don't be late," Von announced as he stood up to leave.

"Thanks, I appreciate that. We'll be there tomorrow."

   After Von and his boy left I went over to the basketball court to watch my brothers play. I could tell they must've had a bet on the game by the way they were playing. We all could hoop and we used our talents to make some extra cash whenever we could. We obviously didn't have the money to pay for a bet if we lost so we made a point to never lose. Once they finished the game, they headed my direction to tell me how it went.

"Yo Tony, we ran them older niggas off the court four times! They hated that we bust they asses in front of they lil' girlfriends so they kept paying for a rematch. Guess how much we just got up out of them?" Byron asked excitedly.

"How much did y'all get?"

"$100! They were mad as hell too! Man today was a good day! We can all get $20 each or we could get $10 each and put 10% into either saving it for a rainy day or investing into something that'll be an asset," said Byron.

I had to smile because although we were poor monetarily, we all had natural gifts that were beyond our control. Byron was the smartest person I knew when it came to numbers and math. He actually enjoyed playing with mathematical equations and percentages. Tevin was the epitome of a technology geek. He could literally break drown any type of technical device and successfully put it back together. He naturally understood computer programming and I'd bet money that he could be the best hacker to ever walk this planet. Jasper and Julian were twins and their gifts were so different. Jasper was super imaginative and creative. He could draw his ass off and draft practically anything; similar to an architect. Julian was the complete opposite. He was more logical and analytical with an obsession for anything regarding criminal justice. This nigga could literally watch shows like *Law & Order* all day and never grow tired of it. Each of us had our own intellectual skills and talents that we brought to the table. As for myself, well I guess you could say I was a master mind. I could basically teach myself anything simply by reading up on it. I was so observant that I could also read people by their body language, energy, what they said, and how they said it. I could pick up on their emotions both sympathetically and empathetically. So what I'm saying is not only did I have a high I-Q but I was also "people" smart.

"Yeah, that's a good idea B. Setting money aside for a rainy day is always smart," I agreed.

"I saw you playing chess with Mr. Big Shot. How did that go?" asked Julian.

"It went even better than expected. I beat him and we had a few words after the game. He was so impressed that he told me to meet him at his restaurant tomorrow. He invited y'all to come too."

"For real, what for?" asked Tevin excitedly.

"It don't even matter what he want. If the nigga wanted me to sell water to a fish I would! Do you know who we talking about Tev? We talking about a man who got money, power and respect! What rock have you been living under?" said Byron.

"Shut up! I'm just asking a simple question. You always have to add yo two cents like you know every fucking thing!" yelled Tevin.

"Calm down y'all! It's not even that deep. I really don't know what he wants but I do know one thing… I'm not missing out on an opportunity of a lifetime," I said as I looked all of them in the eyes.

We all left the park anxious to see what tomorrow would bring. Bryon wasn't exaggerating when he said today was a good day. First, we had the mystery church women who brought us food and books, then we won $100, and most importantly we earned the respect of a man who could put us in a better position regarding our livelihood. I knew in my heart that today would be the last day that my brothers and I would ever struggle.

I couldn't sleep that night because I was too eager thinking about the next day. I tried to relax but it wasn't working so I decided to climb out of bed and do some push-ups & sit-ups hoping that it would help me unwind. Everyone else was still asleep as I finished my last set of reps and gathered my clothes to take a quick shower. As soon as I stepped out of the tub, I suddenly heard footsteps outside of the bathroom door. Since we didn't have a lock on the door, I tried to hurry up and wrap my towel around my waist. Just as I finished, my foster mother swung the door open. From the look in her eyes, I could tell she was high as a kite. I could also tell that she wanted to rip my towel off. I quickly grabbed my clothes and tried to brush past her but she blocked my path.

"What are you doing up so late Tony?" she asked as she looked me up and down in awe.

"None of your business Rachael now move out of my way!" I never addressed my foster mother as "mama" or any other term of endearment. She was no mother of mine as far as I was concerned.

"Oh my, well won't you look at who's all grown up," she groaned as she caressed her lips with her hand.

"I'm not gone tell you to move out of my way again. Now move before I put my hands on you," I claimed through clenched teeth as she continued to inch closer to me.

"I see the way you look at me when my husband isn't looking. I see the look in those pretty grey eyes and I can tell that you want me," she moaned as she traced her finger down my chest.

Just as I began to make my way past her she quickly placed her hand between my legs and grabbed my dick. I was shocked and my initial reaction was to punch her in her shit but instead I pushed her with all the strength in my body. She flew into the bathroom wall and knocked over a vase as she fell to the floor. My foster dad rushed into the bathroom.

"What the fuck is going on here Rachael?" screamed my foster dad Joe as he stumbled into the bathroom sloppy drunk reeking of liquor.

"Nothing honey! I just lost my footing and tripped. Just go back to bed while I clean up this mess. I'll be in there in a second," she said as she rubbed his arm.

"Okay, don't be all night. I got some things I want to do to you," Joe slurred with a smirk on his face. He was clearly oblivious to how much of a whore his wife really was or maybe he was just too drunk to care.

"Oh my, I can't wait! I'll be in there shortly honey."

I rushed back to my room pacing the floor back and forth. I was so angry that tears were rushing down my cheeks. I wanted to punch something. I wanted to scream at the top of my lungs. I just wanted to get as far away as I could from this toxic ass household and never look back. Just as I was cracking my knuckles Tevin woke up.

"What's wrong with you bro? I heard that loud ass bang earlier. You good?" asked Tevin as he rubbed his eye.

"Yeah I'm good. I just tripped in the shower and fell. I'm straight though," I lied as I quickly wiped my tears.

I couldn't fix my mouth to tell him what just happened. I was too ashamed. How could I tell him I'd just been violated by a woman; let alone our foster mother? How could I explain to him that I was aroused and enraged all at the same time? I was confused and I wanted to just sweep this incident under the rug like it never happened. Tevin looked at me as if he didn't believe a single word I had just said but he didn't question me any further. He just slowly nodded his head and went back to sleep.

Now I really couldn't sleep after all of this so I stayed up all night as a million thoughts ran across my mind. I thought about all of the instances where I caught Rachael staring at me or touching me inappropriately and thinking to myself how could I have been so blind to her weird behavior until tonight. The next morning I got up early and went to the kitchen. It was nice to see some food in the refrigerator for a change. I wanted some pancakes and eggs for breakfast but I didn't know a thing about cooking so I read the back of the package for instructions. It took me almost an hour to make enough breakfast for my brothers and the fact that I was being a perfectionist with the measurements didn't make it any better.

After we ate breakfast, we left and went to the park to shoot around until 4:30 pm. It was the summer which meant school was out and we could do whatever we wanted. It wasn't like our foster parents cared about our well-being or whereabouts anyway. It was almost time to meet Von at his restaurant so we left the park and headed that way. Thankfully, it was only like ten blocks away from our house. When we arrived, there were a lot of customers who were either dining or waiting in line to order food. Byron noticed a girl who appeared to be around our age cleaning some tables. She was cute so I could understand why he couldn't help but go over and talk to her. I couldn't hear what was said between them but I could tell she liked him too. He came back to where we were and told us what was said. He got her number and was happy as hell about it too. Just as he was telling us how their conversation went Von appeared from the back office. I noticed that he wore all black again with his jewelry decorating his neck and wrists. He told us to follow him to his office so we did what we were told and followed suit. Once we were inside, there were five chairs posted in front of his desk while his right hand man was standing behind his desk. He too was dressed in all black with a gold chain hanging from his neck. I took a seat first and my brothers followed my lead. Von locked the door to his office and then took a seat at his desk.

"I see you've met my daughter lil man. How did that go?" he asked as he turned his attention to Byron.

"What? I don't know what you talking about," said Byron. I could tell he was nervous and caught off guard.

"You know what I'm talking about. You know the girl named Summer whose number you just got?"

"Oh um, my bad Von. I didn't know she was your daughter. I... huh just thought she was pretty," said B. I had never seen Byron at a loss for words until now.

"I'm gone let you know now that when it comes to the women in my life, I don't play about them. I understand you think she cute and all but don't ever make me show you what I mean when I say I don't play. Understood?" said Von.

"I understand," said Byron.

"So what is it that you want us to do at the restaurant?" I asked while watching Von.

"If you could beat me in a game of chess then you're a fucking genius. I could use some strong mental power on my team. However, what I'm proposing is unorthodox so whatever is discussed in this room is expected to remain confidential."

He switched the hot seat from Byron to me and I felt the heat turning up. I could tell by his tone that whatever he was about to propose was serious fucking business. It didn't matter what he wanted us to do as long as it allowed me to get away from my foster parents and that house.

"I understand. I'm listening," I said.

"So I have a few businesses under my belt but the most lucrative one is the drug game. I sell whatever you can think of; percs, weed, lean, cocaine. Shit you name it I sell it. Business is booming and I'm expanding so I need more workers. If you agree to this deal then I'm willing to pay you and your brothers 1,000 a week." I couldn't believe what I was hearing.

"Is that $1,000 each or altogether?"

"That's $1,000 each weekly." I was excited as hell but I didn't show it.

"Before I make a decision, I need to know the job description first," I announced with my fingers interlocked.

"I already have people to make the products. I just need people to sell it on the corners." I thought about what he said for a moment and then responded.

"I have a suggestion if you're open to hearing it."

"Of course I'm open. What's up lil man?"

"Instead of having corner boys and doing business out in the open, you should sell the product more covert." I was smart enough to know that if we sold drugs on the corner we wouldn't live to see the age of 25.

"I'm listening," said Von.

"By doing business in a concealed manner, you'll practically eliminate attention from the police and enemies. You can accomplish this by using the *Sub Joint* as a front. Do you deliver your subs?"

"Nah, it's been on my mind heavy though. Why?" asked Von as he rubbed the hair on his chin.

"I think you should add delivery to your list of services for the restaurant that way when we deliver your drugs the business disguises it as delivering sub sandwiches instead."

"There's only one problem with that suggestion. Y'all not old enough to drive so how you plan on transporting my shit?"

"That's an easy fix. Buy us some bikes and book bags for us to carry and transport everything. I would even say put the restaurant's logo on the book bags and provide uniforms to make it really look legit." I could see the wheels turning in his mind as I had his full attention.

"Sounds like a plan. We can do this as a trial run for one month and if your suggestions run smoothly, y'all looking at a permanent position on my team," said Von.

Von gave me his number and set up our next meeting time so we could set the plans in motion. After leaving the restaurant we started walking back to our house. I was so excited that I couldn't hold my composure because I knew it was only a matter of time before our circumstances would start to change.

"So what did y'all think about the meeting?" I asked as we crossed the street.

"Shit! I think Von is the man and I wanna be just like him," said Byron.

"Are you sure you wanna do this Tony?" asked Tevin. I thought about what he asked. I felt as though I was faced with two options and both of those options required me trading one devil on my shoulder for another but at the end of the day, I would do anything to get away from Rachel and that house. Tevin just didn't understand my motivation to change our living arrangements. I couldn't keep fighting this battle with Rachel and Joe.

"Yeah I'm sure. This is the first step to a new beginning my brothers. Trust me, I've thought this through."

After we left the meeting we headed back to the house. When we made it there, I was shocked to see that Rachel had made dinner. I've never seen her cook, let alone get groceries to make a meal, but I must say the food smelled delicious. We took our shoes off at the front door and headed to our room. As I removed my jacket, in walks Rachel.

"I hope you boys are hungry. I have the table all set. I was hoping we could eat dinner together for a change."

"I can always eat," said Byron who seemed ecstatic but, I, on the other hand, was uneasy because this behavior was definitely not normal for her. It gave me a weird feeling in my gut.

"Where is Joe?" I asked.

"He had some errands to run but he'll be back later. Why'd you ask Tony?" she responded as she eyed me.

"No reason. I was just wondering."

"Well come and eat before the food gets cold."

After my brothers and I got settled in, we all made our way to the kitchen. I was headed to an open chair next to Tevin when Rachel stopped me in my tracks.

"Actually, Tony I have your seat already picked for you. I know you don't like onions so I made your plate separately. It's the plate next to my chair." She patted the chair next to her as she smiled widely. Again, I had a weird feeling in my gut but I didn't quite understand why.

I took a seat next to hers. It was awkward for me and this nagging feeling in my gut just wouldn't go away. She made chicken breast and pasta with tea to drink. The food was great and I was stuffed by the time I finished eating. After I finished my dinner, I started feeling dizzy and lightheaded. I stood up from the table and stumbled my way to my bed. I heard Jasper ask me if I was okay but I couldn't even answer him. Before I knew it, I had blacked out.

I didn't know how much time had passed as I slowly came back into consciousness but I still felt dizzy as if the room was spinning. My vision was blurry but I could see Rachel on her knees in front of me. My pants and boxers were gone and my body felt stuck as if I couldn't move. However, what I could feel was wetness around my dick. The next thing I knew, the wetness around my dick was gone. As my vision started to focus, I realized Rachael's pale body was hovering over mine. Once I realized she was about to straddle my lap, I reacted and punched her in her mouth. Blood immediately began gushing from her mouth as her body fell to the ground. The last thing I remembered was grabbing a trophy off of my dresser and repeatedly bashing her head until blood covered my body and the walls.

It was as if I was in a horror film when I realized what I had done. My brothers were nowhere in sight. I still felt the dizziness of whatever drug she had given me as I stumbled from the bedroom down the hallway. When I reached the living room, my brothers were all asleep. Tevin was sprawled out across the couch while everyone else was on the floor. I shook each of them one by one until they were all awake. When they noticed the blood on me they started tripping.

"Yo Tony, what the fuck happened to you?" yelled Julian.

"You look like somebody shot you with all that blood on you! What the fuck is going on bro?" yelled Byron.

"Yo, am I the only one feeling nauseous? I feel light headed as fuck," announced Tevin as he rubbed his temple.

"Don't worry about what happened! Let's get the fuck out of here now!" I screamed at them.

I was so distraught that I wasn't thinking rationally. I ran out of the house with blood all over me. The sad thing was no one in this fucked up neighborhood even bothered to ask me if I was okay. It had to have been late in the morning but I didn't care. I ran like a bat out of hell to the only person I knew who could guide me in this type of situation. I ran to the nearest pay phone and dialed Von's number. Surprisingly, he answered immediately. I told him I needed some help. I could tell he knew shit was real by the tone of my voice. He ensured me that he was on his way before hanging up the phone. My brothers finally caught up with me staring me down from head to toe but before they could ask me any questions I whispered, "Don't ask me what happened. I will never speak on what happened so don't even waste your breath." They knew by the look on my face that I was dead serious so they didn't say a word.

Von pulled up in his Range Rover shortly after we got off the phone and scooped us up. I could tell he was immune to situations like these because he didn't even bother to ask me why I was covered in someone else's blood. His only request was for me to sit on the floor of his truck so I wouldn't get any blood on his seats. He took us to one of his apartments and told us to make ourselves comfortable because this would be our new home and we were now family. The next day we started the trial run for delivering the drugs and I must say that shit was a breeze. I didn't like the drug game because of the money. I liked it because I was good at that shit. Von kept his word and paid each of us $1,000 as discussed. That lump sum of money was the first of many and this was just the beginning.

Chapter Two:

Angel

"I don't understand why you can't just go to this charity event with me Tori. The last thing I want to do is go by myself," I said as I searched my closet for an outfit to wear.

"I'm sorry Angel but the last thing I want to do is be around a bunch of uppity ass rich people. That's not my type of scene and you know that. Plus, Shaun is coming over tonight and I refuse to reschedule my dick appointment," laughed Tori.

"They're not uppity. They're just a little arrogant. Come on Tori, you know how my father reacts if I miss a chance to make him look good at his charity event. I'll never hear the end of it. Remember when he threatened to take my car back the last time I missed his gala? Can you just come for me?" I pleaded on the other end of the phone.

"I said what I said. Don't try to guilt trip me into going. You know I've never liked your father and I hate the way he treats you. I understand he's the mayor but when are you going to stop letting him rule every aspect of your life? You deserve to make your own decisions and be happy."

"You're right. I have to go. I need to finish getting ready for this event."

I hung up the phone and continued searching my closet for a dress to wear. I thought about what Tori said and reflected back over my life. My mother died while giving birth to me which ironically happened to be the same way my grandmother died. The women in my bloodline tended to have complications when it came to pregnancy. My father said it was a miracle that I survived so he decided that naming me Angel was befitting. He also told me that the doctors warned my mother that giving birth to me could result in her death but she really wanted to be a mom and this was the furthest she had ever been with a pregnancy without miscarrying. Now that I was in my early thirties, I myself had yet to become pregnant despite the fact that I would have loved nothing more than to become a mother.

My father was relentless when it came to governing every part of my life, even my dating life. I'd only been in one relationship which was with my ex-fiancé Trevor. Our relationship was basically arranged by our parents. After a few years of dating, I actually fell in love with him and we even worked on having children together. That all came crashing down when he claimed that he needed to work late on our anniversary. I figured I'd go to the mall with Tori to buy some new lingerie and find him a gift. Tori and I were joking around and laughing as usual when we passed by a children's store and caught a glimpse of what suddenly made my heart drop. There was Trevor, my fiancé, rubbing on some chick's huge belly while she picked out baby clothes. I also noticed a ring on her left hand. Before I knew it, I had jumped on him and made a scene so bad that the scandal hit the tabloids. Of course my father wasn't too happy about that and he was more concerned about the scandal going public than my heart being broken. It was now over a year ago since our breakup and I was still trying to get over it all.

I finally decided on wearing a gown with a fitted white halter-top and silver jewelry with matching silver heels. I pulled my hair back into a sleek ponytail and applied red lipstick and my signature perfume. I was checking out myself in the mirror when my phone rang.

"Hello."

"Hey baby girl. The event is starting soon. I hope you're ready to smile for the cameras."

"I'm ready Dad, just putting on the finishing touches now."

"Are you wearing the dress I had sent to you?"

"No, Dad. I decided to wear a dress that isn't dated back to the 1950's," I said sarcastically.

"Lose the attitude Angel. I need you to be on your best behavior. I have some very important people coming to donate a lot of money to my organization. Get it together now," he demanded.

"Bye Dad, I'll see you soon." I hung up the phone, grabbed my purse and headed out the door. I despised going to these events.

Chapter Three:

Antonio

I stood in the shower letting the water run down my face and body as I grabbed my shampoo to start washing my hair. After I rinsed my hair and washed my body I stepped out of the shower, grabbed my towel and started drying my hair. I wrapped my towel around my waist and grabbed my wave brush that was sitting on the bathroom counter. Admiring my muscles in the mirror, I applied some wave grease to my fresh fade and started brushing my hair. "Yo boy done fucked around and became a grown ass man!" I thought to myself smiling at my own reflection. There was never a shortage of pussy for me these days. Tall, dark and handsome was how the ladies always referred to me and my grey eyes really made them throw the panties at me. All of my brothers were married with kids except for me. When we were kids we all made a vow that if and when we decided to have a family, we would be the best husbands and fathers we could possibly be because family was so important to us for obvious reasons. However, it was hard for me to trust women so I'd never been in a relationship. I had made it a habit to let women know straight out the gate that I only wanted sex with no strings attached. To me, it was more of a business deal because I kept it strictly business.

I slipped my feet into my house shoes and made my way to the bedroom. I headed towards my walk-in closet to find something to wear for this charity event that I was invited to by a possible connect. Holding business meetings with government officials about the drug game was nothing new for me. These motherfuckers were as crooked as they came but this meeting was different. This was a plot to get out of the drug game. I would be 30 years old soon and shit had definitely changed from when I first started selling. The stakes were too high now. It was time for me to be strictly legit but I refuse to quit until my plans were in motion.

I pulled out an all-black tailored suit with diamond cufflinks, a black tie and my black oxfords. I went over to my jewelry box housing my watch and earring collection and picked one of my favorite black Rolex watches and a pair of black diamond earrings. Next, I grabbed my Ralph Lauren cologne and sprayed it on me. I grabbed my phone to call my brothers and find out where they were because their asses should have been at my house by now. I waited for Jasper to answer the phone.

"What's up big bro?"

"Where y'all niggas at? Y'all should have made it here by now. What the fuck is taking so long?"

"Man that's Byron slow ass. Him and Summer having another argument. I'm outside his crib waiting on him to come out now."

"Where everybody else at?" I said as I grabbed my wallet.

"Tevin said he couldn't make it because TJ has a science fair after school. You know his nerdy ass ain't missing that for nobody. Julian right here next to me in the whip. We just waiting on Byron ass."

"Hold on, let me call Byron. Y'all can just meet us there. I'll go pick his ass up." I hung up the phone, grabbed my car keys and rushed out the front door. I hopped inside my Range Rover truck and pushed the button to bring my shit to life. I waited for Byron to answer the phone since this was my second time calling him. The nigga finally answered.

"Shut the fuck up talking to me! I'm getting sick of this shit for real! Give me my keys back so I can get the fuck out of here!" screamed Byron.

"Yo, just wait outside! I'm pulling up anyway! I'm not trying to break up no fights today!" I screamed at him before he hung up.

When I pulled up to Byron's house he wasn't outside like I told this nigga to do which meant he must be in a heated argument with

Summer again. Fuck! I hate being late to shit and this nigga is wasting my time! I hopped out of my truck and knocked on the front door. I could hear both of them yelling and glass shattering. Byron finally came to the front door with his clothes disheveled and his tie in his hand.

"This bitch won't give me my fucking keys! I swear to God she should have been named Winter 'cause that bitch is cold as fucking ice! I'm getting sick of this shit for real Tony! I can't keep living like this!" he yelled as he jumped in my passenger seat.

"Man just calm down. Y'all always do this break up to make up shit. Y'all gone be back on good terms before you know it."

"Nah, this stress is becoming too much for me. Our relationship is supposed to be my fucking peace! Not my damn headache! Ever since she got that fucking CEO position she been pushing it!"

"Well we got business to handle at this charity event so your drama got to go on the back burner for now."

When we pulled up at the charity event, valet took my keys as we headed inside. Julian and Jasper were already waiting in the lobby for us. We were all dressed to kill in our tailored suits and expensive jewelry. I smiled because I remembered the days when were literally starving. Those were the days that kept us humble because money was no longer an issue for any of us now.

We joked around in the lobby as people began to rush in but one face stood out from everyone else's in the crowd. It was as if they all had disappeared. She was the most beautiful woman I'd ever seen. She wore a white gown that hugged each and every one of her curves. Her full lips were decorated with red lipstick and when her eyes connected with mine, it felt as if I had known her for a lifetime. My eyes followed her every move because I was attracted to her like a moth to a flame.

"Nigga did you hear what I said?" asked Byron.

"Nah, what you say?" I said with my eyes still glued to her.

"I said can I crash at your place tonight but you too busy watching the bitch in the white dress," snarled B.

"What the fuck is your problem? Just because your wife is a bitch doesn't mean every other woman is. Don't call her that," I claimed defensively as if she was already my woman.

"Do you know her Tony?" asked Julian.

"Not yet but I will by the end of the night." My intuition was telling me that this woman was going to be significant in my life in some type of way. I couldn't just let her walk past me without introducing myself. I made my way through the crowd until I was close enough to "accidently" bump into her. I just had to know if her skin was as soft as it looked.

"Excuse me for bumping into you. I can be clumsy at times." She turned around and looked at me with an absolute perfect smile.

"No worries. I can be quite clumsy myself."

"I must say that you look beautiful in this white gown. You really look like an angel. My name is Antonio by the way. I didn't catch your name," I said as I extended my hand to reach for hers. She placed her hand in my palm and spoke as I rubbed my thumb across the back of her hand. It was like an electrical shock between us when we touched.

"Actually, my name is Angel."

"Really? Or are you just saying that to get rid of me?"

"I would only do that if I didn't like your company."

"So you're saying you like my company?"

"Maybe," she answered smiling at me. Just when I was really about to shoot my shot the guy who invited me to the event walked over and patted me on the shoulder grabbing my attention. I excused myself from Angel.

"It was nice meeting you Angel. I'll see you around soon. I have some business to take care of at the moment." She nodded her head and walked away. Her perfume lingered for a moment and I couldn't help but think of how her scent would smell on my sheets. The thought alone shocked me because I had never brought a woman to my house before but here I was imagining her lying naked in my bed.

The entire time during the meeting, all I could think about was Angel. I was just focused on catching up with her before the event was over. I finished taking care of business and now I wanted to see what was up with her. My brothers and I were seated at the bar drinking and talking while I scanned the room for Angel. Byron was still complaining about Summer and what had been going on in their household. I could understand why he was so uptight lately. She basically emasculated him every chance she could.

"I love my boys man but I can't stay in a marriage where I'm miserable and hate going home. Y'all just don't know man," said Byron as he sipped his drink.

"Come on B, is it really that bad to the point where you want a divorce?" asked Jasper.

"Yes! You don't know what it's like to be with a woman that tries to control everything you say and do. Dude she put my boys in water polo. What the fuck is water polo anyway? I wanted them to play football or basketball but she had a problem with that too."

I blocked out the rest of that conversation because I finally spotted Angel's face in the crowd. She was talking to some black dude and I instantly went into territorial mode. I started sizing this dude up. He was short as hell for one; even shorter than Angel. He was dressed well and he wore prescription glasses. I watched their interaction and realized they must already know one another because when he touched her she didn't pull away. However, I could tell she was angry with him by the expression on her face. All of a sudden, some other black woman walked over and interlocked her arm with the guy's. The look on Angel's face seemed as if she wanted to be anywhere but there and I was just the guy to help her out.

"Byron, let me borrow your wedding ring real quick."

"Hell no! The last thing I need is for Summer to bitch at me if I lose my damn ring. She already swears up and down that I'm cheating on her. What the fuck you need my ring for anyway?"

"Don't worry about it. Just give it to me."

B finally gave me his ring after several persuasive arguments on my part so I headed into the direction of Angel. I was about to pull a bold move but fuck it, I'm a bold person. When I reached Angel I kissed her on the check and wrapped my arm around her waist. I could tell she was confused and at a loss for words so I took control of the conversation.

"Sorry I'm late baby. I had to finish up some business at the office." Angel quickly caught on to what I was doing.

"All that matters is that you're here now. I missed you," she smiled at me.

"I missed you too." The chemistry between us was magnetic and I could tell that whoever this guy was that Angel was speaking to could also feel it.

"Who is this Angel?" he asked as he mugged me.

"What's up lil' man. My name is Tony, Angel's husband." I reached out to shake his hand and I could tell that Angel was shocked. So was he.

"Trevor," he replied as he reached his hand out to shake mine. "Funny. Your father didn't mention that you were married," he said as he turned his attention back to Angel.

"When did you speak to my father?"

"Today when he personally invited me to his event. In fact, he told me you were very single and wanted to work things out with me," he said with a sly grin on his face.

"Sorry to disappoint you but her father was misinformed," I said defensively.

"Are you sure about that? I don't see a ring on her finger."

"That's because it's currently at the jewelry parlor getting sized for a bigger diamond. A woman such as Angel deserves the world," I announced as I gazed into her eyes. I meant every word too. "Now if you don't mind, you're getting in the way of me dancing with the most beautiful woman in this entire room." I extended my elbow and she caught the hint interlocking her arm with mine. When we made it to the dance floor I wrapped my arms around her waist and placed my chin between her neck and shoulder. I got lost in the scent of her perfume again as we swayed from side to side. She began to speak after a moment of silence.

"Why did you do that?" she asked.

"You looked uncomfortable like you needed an excuse to leave that conversation. You seemed to be drowning so here I am with my life jacket."

"I can swim just fine on my own for your information. Why are you still playing this role? We can end this game now."

"Something tells me that you don't want to end this game just yet. Something tells me that you're enjoying this just as much as I am."

"What makes you think that?'

"Well the fact that you played along with my game speaks for itself and the fact that you're allowing me to touch you says a lot as well." I ran my hands down her hips and squeezed her thighs. I noticed her breathing changed which meant she was aroused by my touch. I understood that we were in public but I couldn't help myself from caressing her and rubbing every inch of her body. I felt my dick getting hard as I brought one hand just under her breast and bit the side of her neck while pulling her ass closer to my groin with my other hand. She moaned lightly and pushed away from my grip. She practically ran away from me so I ended up losing sight of her within the crowd of people. My brothers approached me talking shit.

"Damn nigga, you damn near raped her on the dance floor. Public affection ain't yo style so she must be something special," Byron joked.

"Move nigga, you in the way! I didn't even get her number yet!" I yelled as I brushed passed my brothers. I ran down the stairs that led to the lobby. When I finally made it outside she was getting inside of a red Mercedes Benz with a license plate that read "4ANGEL." She pulled off before I could even ask her for her number. I immediately pulled out my phone to call Tevin.

"It's the man with a plan. What's up bro?"

"Tev, I need a favor. I need you to look someone up for me. I need their address. I got a license plate number for you so this should be quick and easy." *Wait, what am I doing?* I thought to myself. *Why am I going so hard for a woman that I barely even know?*

"I can do that shit in my sleep. Text me the license plate number and I'll get back to you later. I'm still at TJ's science fair."

"Okay cool. Don't forget bro."

"I'm not. You know I got you."

I went back inside and gave B back his wedding ring. They talked about me for the rest of the event but I couldn't care less because all I could think about was Angel: her voice, her scent, her body and her beautiful smile. She was perfect in every sense of the word and she would be mine whether she knew it or not. Once the event was over, I went back home and patiently waited for Tevin to call me. I was checking emails on my laptop when my phone rang.

"Just the man I wanted to hear from. Tell me something good," I said.

"I see why you keep sweating me. This girl is gorgeous," laughed Tevin.

"Man her looks are just a bonus. Her spirit is beautiful too." The thought of her brought a smile to my face.

"So I just emailed you her address. What's your plan anyway? I know you got one."

"The plan is to accidentally bump into her on purpose again but I have to gather some info first. You know how I do it."

"Yeah I know. I also know you've never had an intimate, personal, romantic relationship with a woman before so my question for you is, is this the beginning of a new relationship?" I thought about what Tevin asked and sadly he was right.

"I don't know. All I know is I can't stop thinking about her and I want to get to know her better."

"Well for you that's major. I'm happy for you."

"Thanks bro," I smiled as I hung up the phone.

Chapter Four:

Angel

"Oh my goodness, Tori you won't believe what happened to me at my dad's event!" I yelled at her as she closed the porch door.

"Well you called me and texted me a thousand times, despite the fact that I told you I had a dick appointment, so I'm assuming this is some serious shit," she said as she took a seat on my sofa.

"Where the hell do I begin? So I get to the event and as soon as I enter the venue this guy, who is very fucking sexy by the way, bumps into me. We had some small talk and then we parted ways." I paused to catch my breath as I paced the floor.

"Okay, what's so bad about that?" asked Tori.

"Let me finish. So I start working the room and guess who approaches me?"

"I have no clue."

"Trevor! All of my emotions of anger and heartbreak came rushing back but I couldn't show him that. Then the bitch he cheated on me with approaches us and wraps her arms around him. I'm livid at this point! I wanted to beat his all over again!"

"So what happened next?"

"Just when I was about to snap on Trevor and his side chick the sexy guy that bumped into me earlier approached us, kissed me on the cheek and introduced himself to Trevor as my husband. Girl I was shocked!"

"Seriously? How does this guy look?"

"He has a beautiful, dark complexion. I mean his skin looked as smooth as butter. He has these striking grey eyes that I got lost in immediately. He's tall and slender; probably about 6'2. He has waves with a connected beard. I mean everything about him screams confident and masculine. The way he speaks, the way he walks, the way he approached me was just so sexy," I said not realizing that I was smiling from ear to ear.

"You look like you in love already!" laughed Tori.

"Shut up! I just think he's different. I wouldn't say I'm in love though. Infatuated? Yes!"

"So what else happened?"

"He put Trevor's ass in his place and then led me to the dance floor. We continued to play the roles of husband and wife while we danced. I could tell he was excited because his dick started getting hard. He was touching me all over my body and I didn't stop him because I can't lie, I was enjoying every minute of it. He pulled me closer to him and bit the side of my neck. It's crazy because his touch felt so familiar like he already knew his way around my body. The next thing I knew I started moaning and had an orgasm in public!"

"Stop lying!" screamed Tori.

"I'm so serious Tori. I was so shook that I had to run away from his ass. The attraction between us was too intense especially since we were complete strangers," I said as I plopped down on my sofa.

"Did y'all even exchange numbers?"

"No, but if it's meant to be then we'll cross paths again."

Chapter Five:

Antonio

I felt like such a stalker waiting outside of Angel's house at six o' clock in the morning. I couldn't sleep because I had been up thinking about her all night. I noticed that she lived in a really upscale neighborhood. This woman had me jumping through hoops already and I didn't even know what the pussy was like yet but I could tell by the way she walked that it was good. I didn't see her car parked in the driveway so I wondered if she was even home. I was just about to pull off when a light came on upstairs. For some reason, I was nervous as if she already knew it was me lurking behind these tinted windows. I waited outside until her garage door opened and she slowly pulled out. I wondered where she was headed this early on a Saturday morning. Was she going to see another man? I pulled off shortly after she did and kept my distance following her until she arrived at a yoga studio. She got out of her car and headed inside the studio as I admired her ass from a distance which was looking nice in those yoga pants. My phone started ringing and suddenly snapped me back into reality.

"Hello."

"What's good bro? I was just checking to see if we're still having that board meeting on Tuesday?" asked Jasper.

"Yeah, you know we have the board meeting every Tuesday unless there's a legit reason to cancel or an emergency where you can't make it."

My brothers and I always held a weekly board meeting to make sure we're all operating on the same page since we knew we were all leading double lives. Jasper had his own architecture company. Byron had his own accounting practice. Julian was a decorated detective for the police department. Tevin had his own IT company. As for me, I had a stream of different businesses ranging from laundromats, vending machines and I even had money invested in the stock market which was basically my passive stream of income. Although I was currently working on a real estate venture, my main focus was on the warehouse where our drug products were packaged and distributed through our shipping company. We all contributed to the warehouse with our specific skillsets. Jasper designed the warehouse and secured it where my brothers and I were the only ones with access to open the building. Tevin installed the high tech computer systems and live video recording that were connected to each of our cell phones. Of course Julian furnished protection from the police department while Byron handled the payroll and bookkeeping by cleaning up our dirty money. I actually managed everyone from the workers to the shipments and the connects we collaborated with for the drugs. The money from the drug game had definitely financed our legit businesses.

"Well Alisha's birthday is this Tuesday so you know I have to do something special for her. Just update me on whatever I miss because I won't be able to make this week's board meeting."

"Taking care of home comes first; a happy wife is a happy life. Tell Alisha I said Happy Birthday."

"I will. Have you heard from Von?"

"Nah, it's been awhile since I've heard from him. You know he's been doing his own thing lately."

"Yeah I know but he been moving real funny here recently."

"I peeped that too but we can discuss this more in person though. I don't like speaking about business over the phone."

"Alright, I'll catch up with you later."

"Okay, cool."

I made a few phone calls to see how shit was running down at the warehouse since I wasn't there. Angel was finally leaving out of the gym after I got off the phone. She jumped back in her car and drove to the grocery store. I thought now would be a good time to "accidentally" bump into her. I checked myself out in the mirror and popped a breath mint before getting out of the car. I felt nervous all over again but here goes nothing. When I walked inside the store she was in the fruit section looking at some organic apples. *Damn, what should I say to her?*

"Don't bite the apple Eve." *Wow, that was real smooth,* I thought sarcastically to myself. She looked over at me and was surprised to see me.

"Wow, if it isn't Mr. Touchy Feely himself," she said as she put the apple down.

"You said that like my touch didn't have you moaning," I said confidently. She didn't respond. She just looked me dead in my eyes. I could tell she was turned on.

"What's your motive Antonio?"

"What do you mean?"

"I mean everyone you encounter has a motive so what's yours?"

"I don't have a motive Angel. I just want to get to know you better. I find you to be interesting," I smiled.

"What if I said I don't find you interesting and don't want to get to know you?"

"I'd say you're lying to yourself. You and I both know there's a strong connection between us. I know you feel it too," I said as I stepped closer to her. She sucked in her bottom lip and walked away. I followed behind.

"Why are you following me?" she asked.

"I'm not following you. I'm just grocery shopping like you are."

We continued talking and shopping for groceries and I couldn't help but want to be around her all the time. She had this chill, laid-back vibe about her despite the fact that she was so beautiful. I don't think she realized just how perfect she truly was. It was time for us to check out and part ways. I could tell she had been heartbroken before and was still protecting her heart by being defensive. However, she was slowly starting to warm up to me as I carried her groceries and walked her to her car.

"You should let me cook dinner for you," I announced as I leaned against her car with my hands in my jogging pants. This sunlight and the summer breeze felt perfect.

"You know how to cook?"

"Yeah, I'm pretty good at it too," I bragged.

"Your girlfriend taught you how to cook?" I smiled at the question. Look at her trying to shoot her shot with me.

"I've never had a girlfriend. I'm the oldest of all of my brothers. I learned how to cook for us when we were kids."

"Really? How many brothers do you have?"

"There's five of us." I felt comfortable enough to tell her a bit about my personal life. Something about her seemed innocent and naïve.

"Wow, I bet that was an interesting household," she smiled.

"Interesting is an understatement. So are you going to take me up on my offer for dinner or what?" She thought about my question and then responded.

"When are you trying to make this happen?"

"How about I pick you up tonight? We can take a walk on the lakefront and then head back to my place for dinner."

"While I actually like the sound of that, there's only one problem," she smiled.

"What is that?"

"I'm a vegetarian so whatever meal you prepare has to be meatless."

"That's easy. I'll let you enjoy the rest of your day and get ready for our date later." We hugged each other and then parted ways. I couldn't stop smiling.

After I left the grocery store I went to the gym to get my work out in for the day. When I finished my workout, I headed back home to clean my house, shower and set out the dinner that I would prepare for that night. I looked in the closet to pick my attire for the evening because I wanted everything to be perfect. I decided on wearing a navy blue button-up, khaki cargo shorts and navy blue Air Max tennis shoes. I wanted to wear something casual since we would be walking on the beach. I was really stepping out of my comfort zone to impress Angel. I would never suggest a date at my place with any other woman but things with her was different. I felt like I already knew her and more importantly, I felt like I could trust her. I told her what time I would be picking her up and pretended like I didn't already know where she lived when she gave me directions. I didn't call her to let her know I was on my way when I left my house because I already expected her to be dressed and ready. I was as happy as a kid in the candy store when I pulled up to her place. I climbed the stairs to her front porch and rang her doorbell. I pulled out my phone and put it on vibrate as I waited for her to answer the door. She opened the door just as I was putting away my phone and I felt a rush of excitement run through my body when I looked at her. I was like a high school teenager with a crush on the most popular girl in school. She stepped out wearing a strapless olive sundress and a statement necklace decorated her neck while her hair was pulled up into a neat bun. She didn't have on any make-up letting her natural beauty stand out on full display. She was like a mystical goddess and I was hypnotized by her vibe.

"You look beautiful," I finally uttered.

"Thank you. You look good too," she smiled at me.

She pulled up her dress slightly to keep it from getting dirty. I reached out my hand for her to hold as we walked to the car. I decided to drive my sedan that night instead of my truck. When we were settled in the car, ironically the song "I Want to Be Your Man" by Roger & Zapp was playing on the radio. I thought it was funny because the lyrics to the song explained exactly how I felt towards

Angel. For the first time with any woman, I actually wanted to be her man. I wanted to be the man who showed her something different. I sung the chorus to her which repeatedly said "I want to be your man (I want to be your man)." She looked over at me and smiled.

"Are you sure about that?" she asked.

"I'm as sure as the sky is blue," I said. She couldn't stop smiling as I continued singing to her.

I pulled into the parking lot of my little get away space since most people didn't even know that the lakefront was actually tucked behind the park. There was a trail leading to the lake that was usually deserted. I hopped out of the driver's side to go open the car door. We held hands as she followed my lead down the trail. We were surrounded by nature and the beautiful and peaceful scenery.

"I forgot to tell you about the steep trail and to wear comfortable shoes. That was my fault."

"It's cool, my sandals are pretty comfortable. This might be a new spot though. It's peaceful out here."

"What's your favorite color?" I asked randomly. I wanted to know everything about her.

"I actually have three favorite colors because I love them all equally: Olive, burgundy and blue."

"That's different. I was expecting to hear pink or purple. You must really love nature then. Every color you mentioned is an earth tone color."

"Yeah, I love being in nature. I can't think of anything more therapeutic and serene than being in this environment," she smiled.

"So you do yoga, you don't eat meat and you love nature? I'm guessing you don't believe in religion either?"

"I'm more spiritual than religious. There's a huge difference between the two. Religion is a tactic to divide and conquer the masses through traditions of it which I don't agree with but I do believe there is a higher power that all man must answer to. Wait, how did you know I do yoga?"

"Lucky guess. You just seem like the type of girl to do yoga. Plus, you look flexible," I flirted.

"Yeah okay, let me find out you've been stalking me," she laughed.

"Trust me, I don't have to stalk." I wasn't going to let her know that I was posted outside of her house like a police officer on a stakeout. I planned on taking that to the grave.

"What about you? Do yo believe in a higher power?" she asked.

"Of course I do. I've read the bible multiple times and believe it wholeheartedly. I refer to him as Elohim or Yaweh. If you haven't read the bible in a while, I suggest you start back."

We continued walking down the trail as we talked and held hands. We spotted a few deer here and there as we got closer to the lake front. She gave me some insight about deer and how they were spiritual animals which made me realize that she was well-versed and could discuss any topic elegantly. It didn't matter if the topic was politics or economics, she was able to clearly articulate her thoughts and teach me a thing or two which I found very attractive. She impressed me because I had never met anyone who actually gave me a run for my money intellectually. Although I was impressed I was also a bit intimated by that because she had the ability to either tear down my world or build it up. When we made it to the sand, she took off her sandals and continued to hold her dress. I watched her as she walked along the seashore and smiled. If she wasn't a goddess, then I didn't know what was. She seemed as fragile as glass; like if a man didn't care for her delicately it would not only shatter her heart but her every being. All I knew was I didn't want to be the man to break her and leave her shattered yet again to put the broken pieces back together.

I walked behind her and wrapped my arms around her waist. She placed her arms on top of mine and rubbed her thump against my hands. Her presence felt like home; like whatever wound I had gathered throughout my life, she had the power to heal. We continued walking and talking until the sun started setting signaling that it was time for us to head back to my place. I kept glancing at her on the ride back to my house. The more time I spent with her, the more my feelings for her intensified. *Is this too good to be true?*

I put my house keys in the lock and pushed open the door as I moved aside to let her walk in first. From the way she scanned the room, I knew she was trying to correlate the things in my house back to my personality. Just from our short time at the lakefront, I knew she was observant like that. Her eyes wandered over every detail before she turned her attention back to me and grinned.

"What does that grin mean?"

"Nothing in particular but I can tell you're materialistic."

"What makes you say that?" I was used to analyzing everyone else so for someone to analyze me for a change was intriguing.

"Everything you own is luxurious; from the cars you drive to the appliances in your home to the clothes you wear. I can tell you find comfort in physical possessions which also tells me that you probably lacked them at some point in your life. Maybe your childhood?" *Damn, she's on point. How did she just read me like a book?*

"Wow, you're good, almost as good as me. I've been paying attention to you too. Your demeanor comes off as if you're naïve and gullible when in actuality you have an inner strength that makes you more than capable of taking care of yourself. You're so in tune with your spirituality that you feel as though you don't belong here. You're a rebel in every sense of the word. You have a big heart which makes you sensitive and I'm willing to bet money that you have a hard time admitting when you're wrong."

"Touché, look at you! I'm impressed! You forgot to describe something else about me though," she smiled as she stepped closer to me. I had my back against the counter in the kitchen. She stepped between my legs and stood just a few inches away from my lips. She wrapped her arms around my waist and looked up at me. Her bright eyes had me mesmerized.

"And what's that?"

"My sexuality," she said seductively. At that moment, her words woke up my dick.

"You enjoy sex but you can't have it with just anyone. There must be an emotional bond there first. Once that bond is established, you are very sexual. You can be submissive in bed but I'm sure you can take control as well. You look innocent but I know you're a freak. Wild and passionate probably describes you best and I'm willing to bet that you orgasm easily too," I smiled. The sexual attraction between us was off the charts. I damn near wanted to skip dinner and make her body my dessert. We stood there staring at each other in silence.

"I want to kiss you," I said finally.

"Why don't you? Are you scared?" she challenged me.

Instead of answering her question, I leaned in and kissed her. Her hand gripped the back of my neck and I noticed that she wasn't wearing any panties when I gripped her ass. I had also already noticed she wasn't wearing a bra when her nipples were hard at the lakefront. She was naked underneath her sundress. I was instantly conflicted because on one hand, I didn't want to fuck her on the first date like I would with any other chick but on the other hand, the sexual attraction was too strong to ignore. My sexual drive for her was animalistic at this point. I pulled her dress up over her waist and reached my hand between her thighs to rub her clit. I eased my finger inside of her and realized two things: she was tight as hell and wet as hell which meant she wanted me just as much as I wanted her.

Although I was conflicted mentally, my anatomy had already made up its mind. My dick was standing at full attention and begging for some loving. I removed her dress tossing it to the floor and bent her over the counter. I kissed her neck and worked my way down her spine as she whimpered. I got on my knees and spread her lips to see how she would taste on the tip of my tongue. Why was I doing shit like licking her pussy while on my knees was beyond me but she was the only woman that ever had that effect on me. I just wanted to please her in any way possible. I continued swirling my tongue around her clit and realized how sweet she actually tasted. I stood up behind her and eased my dick inside of her. Putting on a condom was the furthest thing from my mind because I wanted to feel every inch of her with no boundaries. This was my first time ever going raw because I refused to plant my seed inside a chick that I couldn't care less about. I also didn't usually trust women but every bone in my body told me that Angel was different. She actually gave me a run for my money. Entering her raw was like stepping into another dimension. If I knew pussy could feel this good, I probably would've already had a bunch of kids like my brothers because pulling out might take all of my strength. Her moaning and digging her nails into the back of my leg damn near made me come inside of her so I pulled out.

"Why did you do that," she huffed.

"I don't know if I trust myself," I said as I hovered over her and tapped her lower back with the head of my dick.

"Put it back in," she demanded. I did as I was told and eased my dick back inside of her and bit her shoulder. I had to do something to keep from really moaning. She moaned as I continued exploring every inch of her body.

I was trying to pace myself and take my time but the sensations of her wetness around my dick had me going crazy. She arched her back and threw back her ass to meet each of my thrusts and I knew I couldn't hold back much longer. If her hair wasn't in a bun, I would have had a hand full of it but I settled for wrapping my hand around her neck and gently choking her with enough pressure to let her know she was fucking with a boss. I felt sensations rising within me as if I was on a roller coaster ride slowly approaching the peak to go over the edge. I pulled my dick out just in time and busted on her lower back. I hunched over her to catch my breath and regain my strength because she had me weak in the knees.

After I caught my breath I grabbed a paper towel and wiped her back. She turned around and we stared at each other like two teenagers in love. She inched closer to me and kissed the side of my neck. My dick was getting hard again just from the sight of her naked body. Her body was like a work of art and I didn't mind being her critic. After she kissed my neck she made a trail of kisses down my chest and once I realized she was about to suck my dick my body instantly tensed. I never liked getting my dick sucked because it would bring back the painful memories of my childhood that I had tried so hard to forget. My body felt stuck as if I couldn't move. The memory of being drugged when I was thirteen flashed before my eyes and I was back in that moment of my innocence being snatched away from me. Rachael was hovering over my body once again and all I could think of was how could I protect myself? The color red flashed before my eyes but the screaming of Angel's voice is what brought me back to reality.

"What the fuck is your problem?" yelled Angel as she stood to her feet while rubbing the side of her head. *What the fuck did I do?*

"What do you mean?" I was clearly confused.

"What I mean is why the fuck would you hit me upside my head like that?" She was visibly upset but she still gave me the opportunity to explain myself. *Should I tell her about my childhood? Would she judge me or worst would she even believe me? Will she look at me differently after I tell her I was molestated?* All these questions quickly ran across my mind.

"I'm so sorry Angel. I really didn't mean to hurt you. Are you okay?" I asked as I rubbed her arm.

"I'll be okay but if something is bothering you, you can talk to me about it. I'm more understanding than what you give me credit for Antonio." When she looked at me it was as if she already knew about the skeletons in my closet. Still, I had never opened up to anyone about what happened that night and I wasn't about to now either.

"I really don't feel like talking about it. I'm good now but I do want to make it up to you," I flirted hoping this would distract her.

"You not slick Antonio. I know you're changing the subject but since you're cute, I'll let you get away with it for now. How do you plan on making it up to me?" she asked as she looked me in my eyes.

"Well, first you can start by heading to my bedroom. Lay yo body down on my bed and wait for me there with yo legs spread wide open," I announced as I gripped her ass. My dick was back standing at attention and poking her stomach.

"Don't have me waiting long." She bit my lower lip and then made her way to my bedroom. I watched her in a daze as she walked away.

I went to the fridge and grabbed some whip cream and ice cubes. I also grabbed some chocolate syrup out of the cabinet. There she was laying on my sheets as naked as the day she was born and I couldn't help but smirk to myself because the first thought I had of her when we met was this exact moment. This was manifestation at its finest. All I knew is that I was about to make her body my new home. I had a kinky side to me that most people didn't know about. I had a pair of handcuffs and blindfolds amongst some other sex toys that I would bring out whenever I felt the need and I thought now would be the perfect time to bring them into play. I went to my closet and kept her in suspense about what I was doing.

"Do you trust me," I asked as I grabbed the blind fold and handcuffs out of the box where I keep my kinky shit.

"I trust you. Why?"

"Because I need you to trust me. I said I would make it up to you and I always keep my word." I walked back in the room and placed the items for our sex session on my bed. She looked at me and smiled.

"I trust you. You can do whatever you like to me. My body is now your playground."

She reached her hand down between her legs and rubbed her clit. I could tell she was an exhibitionist because she definitely wasn't shy when it came to her sexuality. I grabbed my blindfold and tied it around her eyes. Next, I grabbed the ice cubes because my shit was starting to melt. I wanted to take my time learning and exploring every inch of her body with her feeling every sensation and enjoying the mystery of what I would do to her next. I grabbed one ice cube out of the cup and traced it from her neck stopping along the way to pay her nipples some attention. Initially, she flinched from the coldness but she quickly got used to it. The sound of her moans was like music to my ears that encouraged me to continue pleasing her. I put the ice in my mouth and circled my tongue around her clit before diving in head first. She rubbed the back of my head and moaned as I inserted my finger inside of her. I peeked up at her to see that her facial expression was scrunched up in ecstasy as she bit down on her lip and rubbed her breast. I wondered if she realized how much of a goddess she was in the bedroom. The ice in my mouth had melted but I wasn't done with my foreplay just yet. I enjoyed licking her. I could have kept my head between her thighs all day, every day. I picked up the chocolate syrup and made a trail from her breast to her mound and licked up every drop. When I stuck my fingers back inside of her she was literally dripping wet. She finally spoke after moaning.

"I want to feel you inside of me," she whimpered.

"How much do you want it?" I asked as I continued fingering her.

"I want it more than anything right now."

"I want to hear you beg for it. Tell me what you want me to do to you first," I demanded.

"I want you to put yo dick inside of me and grind slowly until I come all over it." *Well damn! What man would be stupid enough to let her go? She got my dick leaking without even touching me.*

"Maybe I just want to watch you squirm until you can't handle it anymore," I said as I got on my knees and spread her legs apart. It was like opening the gates to heaven.

"Boy if you don't put yo di…" I shut her up midsentence by finally doing what she had been begging me to do. I put my dick in sliding into heaven on earth.

"Don't call me boy. You fucking with a grown ass man!" I was talking a lot of shit. Probably because I was in my element being in full control. She didn't utter a word. She just moaned and dug her nails into my back. She wrapped her legs around my waist as I continued stroking. I was trying to go slow but I was too excited to take my time. I just wanted to beat it up until it was time for me to pull out. I positioned myself to watch my dick go in and out as I felt that familiar sensation rising within me. *If she hadn't come yet, she better hurry up because I wouldn't be able to last much longer.* My toes started to curl when I felt her muscles grip my dick. It was a mixture of pain and pleasure. It felt like she was scratching the skin off my back and before I pulled out, I felt her juices dripping down my thighs. I came all over her stomach. I felt her legs trembling and my body was stuck. I couldn't move even if I wanted too. I took the blindfold off of her and kissed her on the lips.

"So much for dinner," she said.

"Well, I just had breakfast in bed," I flirted. I finally got up and grabbed a towel to wipe off her stomach. After I wiped her down, I cuddled up next to her wrapping my arms around her.

"Can you scoot over? I'm not trying to lie in this wet spot," she said.

"That was you! You damn near flooded my bed," I laughed.

"Well, that's what happens when you press the right buttons, you damn near got the ocean," she shot back. She traced her fingers along my arm as we cuddled.

It dawned on me that I hadn't asked and her questions about her family, her hobbies or anything that really made her who she was because I felt like I already knew her. "Let's play a game," I suggested.

"What kind of game?"

"Let's play *21 Questions*. According to society, we should have done this before having sex but fuck it. We can dance to the beat of our own drum. You can go first."

"What are your parents like?" she asked. I instantly thought about Rachel and Joe and the painful memories of my childhood came rushing back.

"I don't know about my biological parents but my foster parents were an abusive, white couple. I don't have anything nice to say about them so I rather not say much else."

"So you were adopted? What about your brothers?"

"We were all adopted by this white couple when we were infants. We grew up together and bonded as if we were blood related. They are my 'brothers from unknown mothers' and I love them like they were my blood." I don't know why but I was getting very emotional. She brought up feelings inside of me that I never realized I had before.

"Wow, I can't even imagine what you must have gone through with that couple. Unfortunately, everyone isn't cut out for parenting."

"What are your parents like?" I asked her.

"I never met my mother because she died while giving birth to me. I myself almost didn't survive so it's a miracle that I'm even here; hence the name Angel. My dad is overprotective and over-bearing but he did raise me by himself and I am grateful for that. I'm the only child."

"That sounds like a lonely childhood," I said.

"Yeah, it was lonelier than you realize. What do you do for work?" *Damn she's asking all of the hard questions right out of the gate.*

"I'm a jack of all trades and a master of them all. I have a few businesses that I own and manage. One of them being a few laundromats but I'm looking to get into real estate. What do you do?" A part of me wanted to be honest about the drug game but what was the point when I'd be leaving that lifestyle soon anyway.

"I'm a child psychologist. My dad really wanted me to go to school for something more prestigious but I love kids and more importantly, I love helping them heal."

"What made you decide to go that route?"

"I believe this occupation called me to go this route because we never truly realize how so much of what happens in our childhood is a direct correlation to how we act as adults." This peaked my attention because it explained why she was so observant and I couldn't help but feel as though we had met for a specific reason.

"Explain what you mean by what we encounter in our childhood is a direct correlation to our adulthood."

"So let's say you were neglected by a parent as a child. As you grow, you may consciously forget about being abandoned but your subconscious mind never forgets. As a result, you may actually encounter relationships in your adulthood where you're attracted to a partner who triggers your childhood wounds in order for you to heal."

"Damn, that's deep. I never thought about psychology from that perspective. If you love kids so much how come you don't have any? I'm surprised you don't have any at your age, and I'm going to guess and say you're 30."

"I'm 32 actually. It's not like I never tried to have kids. The women on my mother's side of the family have a hard time with pregnancy. We either miscarry or unfortunately, can't get pregnant at all. I still want kids though," she said as she rubbed my hair. It was something about her touch that was so relaxing. I wanted to ask her some more questions but before I knew it, I had fallen asleep.

The next morning, I woke up to her beautiful face resting on my chest. I lifted the covers slightly and realized we both were still naked. I slowly eased from her embrace careful not to wake her. I went to the bathroom to take a quick shower and wash my face before going to the closet to put on some pajama pants. I set the matching top on the bed for her to put on whenever she decided to wake up and I went to the kitchen to get breakfast started. I was starving since we skipped dinner last night. I decided to make some banana and strawberry crepes, scrambled eggs, turkey sausage links and some mixed fruit on the side. I was flipping over the sausage links when she wrapped her arms around my waist and placed her face in the middle of my back. I could get used to her touch and I could tell she loved physical affection.

"Whatever you're cooking smells really good; except for the sausage," she chuckled.

"I know but the sausage is for me though. I know you don't like it," I said as I turned the heat down a bit.

"I like this sausage though," she said as she squeezed my dick.

"Whoa, don't start nothing if you don't plan on finishing it," I flirted as she planted kisses on my back.

"Who said I wouldn't finish it?" she asked as she reached her hand inside of my pants and stroked my dick.

Her sexual appetite was something serious. I loved it though as I turned around to face her. She had fixed her hair into a neat bun and was wearing my shirt. She looked sexy in my clothes but all I wanted to do was rip it off. She started kissing my neck again and I could tell she wanted to give me head. This must have been a fetish of hers but I didn't want a repeat of yesterday. I still didn't understand how I had blacked out and hit her because I had no recollection of any of it. When she started kissing down my chest I stopped her and acted like I was distracted cooking breakfast. I could tell she was frustrated but I didn't know what else to do. I finished cooking and fixed our plates. We sat at the table and sparked up a conversation.

"You got any plans for the day?" I asked.

"Yeah, I have brunch with my dad in a few hours and then shopping with my girls." I could tell she was still irritated from earlier but I just ignored it.

"You have brunch with your dad?" I repeated what she said out loud for her to hear the words she just spoke. "I hate to say this but I don't think I'm going to like your dad." I said in a matter of fact tone.

"You wouldn't be the first person to not like him. None of my friends like him either but I think he feeds off of that in some twisted way. You have any plans on this beautiful Sunday?" she asked as she ate her fruit.

"I'm going to hoop with my brothers and check on my businesses later. Other than that, I might just chill. You can spend the night again if you want." I was hoping she would agree to it because I wanted to wake up with her next to me again.

"I'll think about it," she smiled.

She left shortly after we ate breakfast and I missed her as soon as she was out of my sight. I didn't want her to leave in the first place but she stressed that she couldn't miss brunch with her dad. I hadn't even met this dude but I didn't like him already. I didn't like how he kept a tight leash around her neck like she wasn't a grown ass woman. I could see that Angel was going to need a backbone when it came to dealing with her father and I would gladly be that force to help her with that. I went to my closet to pack my bag and head to the basketball court to meet my brothers but I thought about Angel and the time we shared thus far as I went about my day.

Chapter Six:

Angel

I thought about Antonio as I drove to meet my dad for our usual Sunday brunch but first I had to run home to shower, change and feed my puppy. Every time he crossed my mind, there was a huge grin on my face. However, that grin disappeared once I entered the restaurant and seen the look on my dad's face. He was clearly upset and he didn't even stand to greet me when I made it over to the table. As always, he looked pristine and presidential just in case paparazzi were to catch him out and about.

"You're late Angel. I've been waiting here for over twenty minutes. A courtesy call would have sufficed."

"Well, I was busy dad," I announced as I took a seat sitting my purse beside me.

"Were you busy with that hoodlum Trevor told me about? I didn't realize you were a married woman. I sure as hell never got that memo," he said sarcastically.

"Speaking of realizations I didn't realize that I wanted to 'work' things out with Trevor. Last time I checked, he was married to the woman he cheated on me with, remember?" I fired back.

"Honey, men have been cheating since the beginning of time and I doubt that will ever change. Trevor is a good fit for you. When will you get that through your head?" he said as he wiped his mouth with his napkin.

"No. What you meant to say is Trevor is a good fit for you and your image, not mine. Is this why you wanted me to come here so you can control me as if I'm a puppet on a string? I could have stayed where I was."

"So you were with that hoodlum? Antonio is his name right? I hope you know him as well as you think you do."

"I'm sure I know more about him then you do," I said defensively.

"So you must already know about him being a big time drug dealer who's been on the government's radar for a while now?" he said with a devilish grin on his face.

"Wow! I would have never thought you would stoop so low to make up rumors about someone that you barely even know." I was getting angrier by the second.

"Don't be silly Angel. You know I don't spread rumors but I do spread facts." He handed me some documents and pictures of Antonio that confirmed his allegations. To say that I was at a loss for words was an understatement. I was furious. How could Antonio just lie to my face like that?

"What's the point of showing me this? I find it quite funny that you couldn't wait to dig up some dirt on Antonio. Trevor must really be intimated by him," I said as I shoved my dad's evidence back across the table.

"I'm showing you this because we both know, for whatever reason, you really like this guy but I'll be damned if I let you or anyone else for that matter destroy the life I've worked so hard to build. This is fair warning for you to leave this hoodlum alone. He's nothing but trouble and you're too good for him." I grabbed my purse and stood up.

"Brunch was nice, dad. It was good seeing you."

He called after me but I continued walking away. I had learned over the years that I couldn't show my father what cards I held; it was best to keep him guessing. I was fuming as I hopped in my car and headed straight to Tori's house. I didn't want to speak to Antonio right away because if I did, I would have certainly blown up on him. My emotions were all over the place as I knocked on Tori's door. I wanted to get her perspective on things since she had a different upbringing than I did. While I was brought up in an upper middle class family, she grew up in the projects and even stripped to pay for college. How did we become friends you ask? Well, we pledged together back in college. She was actually my sorority line sister and from the moment we met, we just clicked. I even had a bit of a ratchet side now. She finally swung open the door.

"Girl, why the hell you knocking on my door like the police? You don't do that in the hood Angel. That's the knock when yo ass is about to go to jail," she complained as she tied her robe. Usually, I would laugh at her shenanigans but this time I brushed past her without even cracking a smile.

"Am I interrupting something? Is Shaun here?" I asked as I sat on her couch.

"No, he just stepped out. What's going on? Did something happen with Mr. Chocolate?" Tori asked as she joined me on the couch.

"His name is Antonio and yes a lot has happened since we last spoke. Let me bring you up to speed real quick. While I was at the grocery store we crossed paths again. He asked if we could take a walk on the beach and then head back to his place for dinner. We did that and it was one of the most memorable dates I've ever had. I mean everything with him was perfect. We go back to his place and we end up having sex which I must say, was the best I've ever had. So I just left brunch with my dad and he's already rooting against Antonio. He gave me some documents showing that Antonio was being investigated by the government for drug trafficking. My dad basically threatened me to leave him and now I'm angry at Antonio for lying to me and making me look stupid," I said in haste.

"Girl fuck yo dad! He's a pompous asshole that no one likes anyway so regardless of who you date, if it ain't Trevor then they'll never be good enough for him. As for Antonio, I think you should speak to him and get the real scoop on that drug trafficking shit. You must really care about this nigga. You don't think y'all are moving too fast?"

"The connection I have with him is hard to explain. It doesn't feel like we're moving too fast because it's like we already know each other. How can we be moving too fast when the connection we have is timeless?"

"Wow that was real sentimental. I felt that in my heart when you said that."

"I'm being serious Tori. I don't want to let him go just yet. I have feelings for him. Like damn it, I'm already emotionally involved with him."

"Damn, he put it on you like that? Welcome to the 'addicted to the dick' club. Now you see why when Shaun calls, I'm running like a crackhead to the drug dealer!" laughed Tori.

"Damn can you be serious for five minutes?" I yelled at her.

"My bad girl, I'm just in a goofy mood. If you don't want to let him go, then don't. It's really that simple. Fuck yo daddy and continue to see Antonio. He might end up being yo new daddy," she laughed again. I grabbed my purse and stood up to leave her ass too.

"Bye Tori! I'll call you when you grow up tramp."

"Bye tramp! You got this! You already know what you want to do anyway! I don't know why you asking me for advice! You know I'm not good at this shit!" she yelled as I headed to my car.

I was confused and didn't know where to go when I got inside the car. Should I head back to Antonio's house and address this bullshit head on or should I leave him alone like my father wanted? I was just angry at the fact that Antonio lied so easily when I clearly asked his ass what he did for work. One thing I didn't like were liars so I decided to go to his place and confront him because I definitely wasn't the passive aggressive type of person. Whenever I had some shit to say, I would just speak on it. I refused to call him and tell him exactly what was going on. I wanted to look him in the eyes when I dropped this bomb on him. When I did make it to his house, I continuously knocked on his door until he opened it. He was shocked to see me upset. He poked out his lips for a kiss but I walked right passed him leaving him hanging.

"Well hello to you too," he said sarcastically.

"Is it always this easy for you to lie to someone's face?"

"What are you talking about Angel? How about you stop beating around the bush and get to the point of this temper tantrum you're obviously having?" he said as he we walked away. I was hot on his trail.

"What I'm talking about is you lying to my fucking face about your occupation. I find it funny that you left out the fact that you're a fucking king pin!" His nonchalant attitude was starting to piss me off.

"Are you done tripping? I'll gladly clarify some shit for you but not until you calm the fuck down," he announced as he sat on his bed. I closed my eyes and took a couple of deep breaths to reclaim my emotions. When I opened my eyes, I noticed he was shirtless with just basketball shorts on. He looked so fine. I liked the way he's handling this. I'd be lying if I said it didn't turn me on.

"Why did you lie to me Antonio?" I finally asked.

"First let me ask you this and then I'll answer your question. How did you even get that info on me?" He was calm and logical under pressure. I guess he was revealing a different side of himself.

"My father is the mayor. He investigates any and everyone who comes close to me. He's controlling like that. He told me that you were a drug dealer and to basically stay away from you."

"Interesting. I didn't lie to you I just withheld that part of my life since I'm working on some ventures to get away from that lifestyle. I didn't want you judging me like you're judging me right now."

"I'm not judging you but I am wondering why you're apart of destroying families by pumping drugs into communities when you know exactly what a broken home feels like?" I regretted those words as soon as they left my lips.

"Wow! See this is why men don't open up now! As soon as we do, y'all throw that shit back in our faces and if you really wanted to know some shit about me you would ask me instead of assuming!" he yelled.

"I'm sorry. I didn't mean what I just said." I responded as I sat next to him on the bed.

"You don't know what I went through in my childhood and you didn't even give me the opportunity to tell you about it Angel. I've been through some shit, okay? I didn't grow up with a silver spoon in my mouth like you. Do you know what it's like to not know where your next meal is coming from? When I was younger, I seen an opportunity to better me and my brother's circumstances so I took it and ran with it. I'm not proud of it but I did what I had to do and I don't regret it. What makes me any different from a doctor prescribing drugs? Shit the pharmaceutical companies are the biggest drug dealers of all time so tell yo pops, if he really want to investigate some shit, that's where he should start!" He was so angry that I decided just to let him vent. I could tell he was used to bottling up his thoughts and emotions. Maybe I had just triggered some things inside of him when I made my statement? I still didn't want him to be upset with me for saying it though and I must admit that he did make some valid points too.

"You're right and I apologize for hurting you. That was never my intention," I said as I rubbed his back.

"I don't open up easily and I damn sure don't trust just anyone Angel so if I do open up to you, don't make me regret that shit."

"I understand and I won't take for granted your trust," I meant every word too. I felt bad about jumping to conclusions and not giving him the benefit of the doubt. I had a bad habit of assuming and I knew it was something I had to work on.

We sat in silence as I continued rubbing his back. Even though he lied to me, I understood why and it didn't change the way I felt about him. If it had been anyone else, I would have ended the relationship instantly but I got the feeling that even if I did leave Antonio something would pull me right back to him. Although we just had our first argument, it seemed as though it had brought us closer together in some weird way. My head was resting on his shoulder as I continued rubbing his back. I started kissing his neck and rubbing his thigh. I could tell that he was still upset but he was also aroused by my touch. He didn't stop me when I reached inside of his basketball shorts and rubbed his dick until it hardened. When I looked at him, his eyes were closed as he bit his lower lip. I wanted to get on my knees and feel him inside of my mouth but I knew from experience that he had issues with receiving head. I wanted to ask him about that but I didn't think the timing was right. I figured he would eventually bring it up when he was ready to discuss it. He leaned over and kissed me as he laid me on the bed and climbed on top of me. He ran his hands up my thighs and pulled down my panties throwing them to the floor. He planted kisses and bite marks on my inner thighs before diving in head first. I could feel the warmth of his tongue. It felt like it was made just for me. I started moaning and rubbing my hands through his hair as he gripped my hips. Just when I was about to come, he stopped and stood up. He took off his basketball shorts and grabbed me by the ankles pulling me to the edge of the bed. In one quick motion, he slid his dick inside of me as I put my legs over his shoulders. His stroke was fast and hard as if he was trying to punish me for pissing him off. He was being rough with me but I was turned on by his dominant nature. We both moaned as we watched his dick slide in and out of me. His moan was so sexy. As always when I come, I dig my nails into whatever I can get my hands on and the closest thing to me were his legs so I dug my nails into them as I closed my eyes and relished in the sensations that rushed through my body. He pulled out shortly after and came on my stomach before collapsing on top of my body while breathing heavily.

"Fuck," he said as he struggled to catch his breath. I circled my fingers all over his back as he laid there tiredly.

"I'm sorry," I said again as I looked him in his eyes.

"It's cool. Just don't let it happen again," he said as he kissed my lips.

He got up to go get a towel while I admired him from afar as he walked around naked. He was impeccable in every since of the word. Although we were sexually compatible, we were also mentally and spiritually compatible which were just as important to me. When he returned I couldn't stop smiling at him. He caught a glimpse of me staring at him as he wiped me down and smiled too.

"Why are you smiling so hard?" he asked.

"I'm just mentally thanking the creator for the parents who made you," I flirted.

"If I ever had the opportunity to meet them I would thank them too," he announced as he cuddled up next to me.

We decided to watch a comedy show and relax in each other's embrace. I caressed his hair and neck as he laid between my legs and rested his head on my pelvic. I felt a surge of electricity run through my body as he gently rubbed his thumbs up and down my hips. We never declared a title for whatever bond we shared. All I knew was that whatever this thing was between us, I wanted it every day for the rest of my life.

Chapter Seven:

Kenneth

Every time I seen my son, my heart would start racing uncontrollably and my guilty conscious would rear its ugly head once again. I had been running from my conscious since the dreadful day when I realized how my selfish actions had finally caught up with me and I could no longer escape the consequences. When I was a senior in high school I met a girl who was the most beautiful creature inside and out. I would sneak to the park to play basketball with my friends when one day I noticed her sitting on the bench with a notepad. Something told me to go find out more about her and the moment I did my life was never the same. I felt a sudden rush through my veins when she gazed into my eyes to tell me she was writing poetry. Everything about her captivated me. She was brown skinned with a big curly afro and delicate facial features. I found out that she was also a sophomore and by her shy nature I could tell she was a virgin which only drew me in that much closer. Against my father's wishes, I started going to the park every day after school just to spend time with her. I wanted every waking second spent with Angela.

My father was a lieutenant general for the U.S. Army so to say he was strict was an understatement. He was abusive and extremely controlling to the point where my mother was afraid to leave him. We lived in constant fear and I took every opportunity I could to get away from him, which is why I would often escape to the park after school while he thought I was in tutoring. Angela and I developed a strong bond spending those afternoons together after school. She attended public school while I was privileged enough to go to a private school. She had a single mother who worked second shift so we were able to spend a lot of alone time together after school. Although we were from different backgrounds, we had a lot in common and were similar on every level possible. One day after school I walked her home like I had always done but this time was different. She invited me inside to stay for a while. I had never pressured her to invite me inside even though it was hard to resist since we were sexually attracted to one another. Once we got inside, we headed straight to the bedroom. I sat on her bed as she got comfortable and took off her shoes. She walked over to sit beside me and just looked at me. She still seemed shy as she continued to undress. Although I was senior, I was still a virgin as well and was actually nervous to have sex for the first time. I was also apprehensive because I knew I would be leaving for college soon and didn't want to start something with her. However, I couldn't help the fact that I was magnetically drawn to her. She was left in nothing but her bra and panties and I couldn't help but stare at her. It was as if she was glowing when she took off her clothes. She ended up losing her virginity that night and from that day on I would meet her at her place to have sex whenever we could. We continued our relationship even after I left for college. I would often come home just to be with her.

While I was still a student in medical school we found out she was pregnant. I was both excited and scared but I still wanted to keep this news away from my father. Out of excitement, I told my mother who ended up telling my father about Angela's pregnancy. When he found out, he went ballistic on me. He even gave me money to force Angela to get an abortion. I took the money and pretended like I was going to use it for an abortion when I really used that money along with my refund check from school to rent an apartment for Angela and our future family. I was in class when she called to tell me she was going into labor. I rushed back home and made it just in time to see my son being pushed out her womb. He was the most beautiful baby I had ever seen. He had bright grey eyes just like me and was constantly smiling. I could tell he was going to be a very happy baby. He would wear his dark skin as a badge of honor I thought to myself as I held him in my arms. I stayed with Angela and our son for the remainder of their hospital visit before returning back to school. I would call and check on them daily but I could tell that the long distance and her role as a single parent was starting to take its toll on both her and our relationship. I would often send my best friend Greg to our apartment to help her out whenever he could but he could only help so much since he was just starting his career as a police officer.

Greg had warned me on a few occasions that Angela was slowly changing for the worst. He told me that when he would visit, my son would smell like he hadn't bathed in days and his diaper always seemed full as if it hadn't been changed. He even told me that Angela would forget to feed him from time to time and would refuse to bond with him neglecting his basic needs. Usually I would be home to visit but my father kept me extremely busy helping him organize his high profile events whenever I wasn't at school. It was like he knew Angela was at her breaking point and needed me the most. Unfortunately, I didn't realize this until it was too late. I was attending one of my father's heavily publicized events when he introduced me to a woman who he felt would be a great wife for me. Little did he know, the only woman that I could see as my wife was Angela and I planned on making that happen as soon as I was no longer under his grip. I took a few photos with this mystery woman just to get him off my back. I had forgotten my phone in the car so when I left the event, I realized I had a ton of missed calls from Angela. I called her back but she never answered. I suddenly had this feeling in the pit of my stomach that something was terribly wrong but I had to head back to school if I wanted to make it time for my United States Medical Licensing Examination. I need to take this exam if I was going to become a medical doctor. As I was leaving the exam my phone rang. It was my guy Greg.

"Hello?"

"Kenny are you sitting down right now? If not, you might want to take a seat for this."

"I don't like the sound of this. What's going on?" I asked frantically.

"I don't know how to say this but it's Angela. I received a call from the dispatchers about a foul odor in your apartment complex. Angela is gone Kenny."

"Do you mean gone like missing or gone like I won't ever see my baby alive again?" I asked as I waited for his response in agony.

"I mean gone like you won't ever see her alive again. I'm so sorry for your loss," he said. I could tell he was emotionally overwhelmed. My heart instantly ached as I digested his words and reality sank in. I broke down and sobbed uncontrollably. I yelled as I held the phone against my ears and barely heard Greg's voice on the other end of the phone.

"Kenny it gets worst... your son is missing too. You need to get your ass here as soon as possible!"

When I finally made it to our apartment, I immediately smelled the overwhelming odor of a body that had been deceased for days. I noticed that everything I had bought my son was gone. It was as if there was no trace of him ever being in our home. I went to the bedroom and discovered a letter that was written by Angela on the dresser. I was already an emotional disaster but the letter brought me to my knees.

"Dear Kenneth,

I want you to know that my love for you is unconditional, limitless, and has no boundaries. Although my love for you is limitless, I've never felt so alone in my life. I needed you here to help me with our son. I needed you here to help me battle my demons. Where were you when I needed you? I've been battling depression and my inner demons to hurt myself or worst hurt our son. When my thoughts constantly started governing my actions to harm our own flesh and blood, I decided to place him in the hands of someone who could better care for him. He deserves to live.

P.S. I saw you and that woman in the newspaper. Is she your new lover? If being with her is what makes you happy then be with her. I still love you and always will."

I wiped the tears from my eyes as I sat on the bed. How could I have been so selfish? I was so busy trying to build a foundation for my family that I neglected them in the process. It felt as if regret, shame and guilt had smacked me in the face all at once. If Angela only knew that she was the only woman I had eyes for. If she knew that I wanted to spend the rest of my life with her she would have never killed herself. I lost everything I loved in the blink of an eye. The love of my life had killed herself and I had no clue who had my son. How would I ever be able to recover from such a tragedy?

It had been a few months since Angela's death and I still hadn't found my son. It was like he never existed. Finding him was the only thing keeping me sane. I moved on with my life but it felt like I was on auto-pilot. I was just going through the motions. Gradually, the years passed by but I never gave up searching for my boy. I prayed every day that I would eventually find him. Although I had everything I could ask for materialistically, it was pointless because my family wasn't here to share it with me. My hopes of finding my son were starting to fade until Greg, who was now a seasoned detective, called me up.

"Kenny, are you sitting down right now? If not, you might want to take a seat for this," said Greg. It was déjà vu all over again.

"I can't handle any more bad news Greg."

"This is the best news I could ever tell you my friend so hear me out."

"I'm listening," I said reluctantly.

"The other day when I dropped my son off at the park to shoot some hoops, I noticed this kid sitting at a picnic table. He happened to be playing chess with a suspect I've been investigating for years now. What caught my attention about the boy were his eyes, complexion and age. He left shortly after I dropped off my son and I didn't get as good of a look as I wanted so I decided to go back to the park the next day to see if he would be there again. When I went back he was there and this time he was playing chess by himself so I decided to go over and join him. When I sat across from him and looked him in the eyes I knew I had finally found your son but first I wanted to be 100% sure before mentioning this to you so I decided to follow him home one day. He had four other boys with him when I tracked him down. I identified the owners of the home in our database at the office. It turns out that he was adopted by a middle-aged couple just days before Angela's death." I was speechless. I was so filled with joy that I didn't know what to say.

"I have the address for you. We found him Kenny. We finally found him," announced Greg.

My emotions were scattered as I wrote down the address. What do I say to a 13-year-old boy? What if he asks about his mother? What if he wants nothing to do with me after I tell him the truth? My guilty conscious was haunting me again. There wasn't a single day where I didn't think about what I could have done differently. I always thought to myself about what would've happened if I had only answered the phone that night.

The next morning, I put my pride to the side and made my way to the address that Greg had given me. I found myself mentally rehearsing the words I would say to my son. The closer I got to the house the more I became a nervous wreck. I noticed that the home was in a poor neighborhood that was riddled with crime and filth. Here I was living a life of prosperity that was laced with lavish things and my seed was living in the worst conditions. Regret and guilt slapped me in the face once again as I pulled up to a raggedy single-family home that was in need of some serious home improvements. I shut off my car and sat for a second as I contemplated my next move. Just as I reached for the door handle, my son stepped outside holding a board game. There were four other boys with him all wearing clothes that resembled rags. I could tell that they were being neglected but this was probably considered normal in this neighborhood. The boys continued down the block with one of them holding a basketball. I started my car and followed them to a park not far from the house. The other boys went to the basketball court while my son sat at a table and played chess by himself. It was at that moment when I realized that my son must have been pretty smart which didn't surprise me because his mother was extremely gifted intellectually. She was literally the smartest woman I had ever known and that still hadn't changed.

I finally got the courage to get out of the car and approach him but first I decided to put on my sunglasses and a baseball cap as a disguise. The closer I got to him the more I realized that he looked just like me. I had tears in my eyes as I stood just a few feet away from him. He was so focused on the chess game that he didn't realize I was standing right in front of him. I cleared my throat to erase the emotions that would cause my voice to shake. He looked up at me when he heard me.

"You want to play?" he asked.

"Sure but I got a feeling that you're pretty good at this though," I said as I took a seat across from him.

"Let's just say I've never lost a game and probably never will," he boasted. Look at my boy.

"I can tell you're really smart. You must read a lot of books."

"Yeah most definitely. I'd rather read a book instead of watch TV any day. Martin Luther King Jr. said a mind is a terrible thing to waste and I believe that whole heartedly," he announced.

"You're a wise young man with a very old soul and as long as you put your mind to it, you can accomplish anything."

"Thank you. I really appreciate that," he smiled.

I had become very emotional and was about to break down and cry. I still couldn't tell him that I was his father. I felt more comfortable just being in his presence and watching over him from afar. Although he looked just like me, he behaved more like Angela. She was very philosophical, poetic and spiritual. She embodied each of those aspects and applied them to her every being. I could tell by the way he spoke that my boy was just the same.

We continued talking and playing the game. By the end of it, I realized that my son was such a gifted child and I was grateful to be his father. After the game, I pulled my wallet out of my pocket and handed him some money. At first he refused to take it but he finally gave in when I insisted. I stood and reluctantly left him at the park. I called Greg and asked him to covertly install a camera system in the house so I could keep a close eye on my boy. I started shadowing him from a distance as he grew older. I was present at all of his basketball games, graduation and every other important milestone in his life. As he grew into a young man, I noticed he was headed towards a lifestyle that I didn't necessarily agree with. Despite my disapproval, I let him live his life without interjecting because I knew he was more than capable of protecting himself. I hoped and prayed that eventually I would get the courage to reveal myself to him.

Chapter Eight:

Von

"Hey baby girl. What's been going on back at home?" I asked as I held the phone against my ear counting my money.

"Byron and I have reached our breaking point. There is no more love in this relationship daddy. I can't keep going through this," complained Summer.

"Summer, I need you to string him along for as long as you can. I got some shit in the works." I was watching my surroundings like a hawk as I sat in my truck. Since I had become a federal informant, I was relocated to an unknown location. This informant shit had me super paranoid with everything and everyone.

"I don't want to be with him anymore dad! I don't want to play this game! I'm in love with another man and I want to build a life with him! This bullshit is getting in the way of that!"

"Shut up with all that bullshit you talking about Summer! If it wasn't for me you wouldn't be rocking that expensive ass wardrobe you love so fucking much or driving that damn BMW that got you sitting pretty! You love all this shit that comes with this lifestyle! It just comes at a price though! Now do what the fuck I said and string his ass along until I say so! I gotta run but keep me posted on his every fucking move and try to get your hands on his bank account information. I'm running low on my funds."

"And how the hell do you expect me to string him along when I don't even want him near me?"

"You have a vagina right? If you have to, use your womanly assets. Everybody knows that good pussy is blinding. Look, I don't really care what you do. You're smart so figure it out!" I snapped.

"You owe me big time for this one and I want my share of your cut!" she yelled on the other end of the phone.

"You already know I plan on lacing yo pockets so I don't know why you even fixed yo mouth to say that shit. I gotta go!" I announced as I hung up. I was rolling my blunt when my burner rang.

"Talk to me." I said as I continued rolling my blunt.

"Is everything going as planned?"

"Yeah, everything is falling into place as we speak. Once I knock over one domino it'll all come tumbling down. It's just a matter of time before shit hits the fan."

"I love the sound of that. Just stay under the radar until the dust settles and then you'll get your money."

"That's what I'm talking about! Say no more," I said as I hung up the phone and lit my blunt.

As shit was starting to hit the fan, it began to feel like the walls were closing in on me. All of the fucking dirt I'd done back in the day was starting to catch up with me. When I was fresh in the game, I had to establish a name for myself. I couldn't play pussy in a lifestyle like this. You were either respected or disrespected; kill or be killed. Obviously, I was still standing in the drug game decades later so you know the dead bodies had piled up over the years. Not to mention, I was running low on funds so this shit was becoming depressing. I should have listened to Tony when he told me how to invest my money and flip it but my pride and the underlying hate I had for this nigga ran too deep. When I took in him and his dusty ass brothers, I didn't expect for this nigga to take over my organization the way he did. Everybody ran to his ass for advice on every fucking thing! Even my right hand man started riding his dick like he was God! It was as if I didn't exist when in actuality I was the one who started this shit from the ground. It would be a cold day in hell before I let him take over everything I had worked so fucking hard for!

Loyalty, honesty and trust were the three biggest traits that Tony expected from both his workers and his brothers and so far his drug cartel had been running smoothly without a fucking glitch. In order for me to tear down his organization, I had to attack it from within. I couldn't attack it directly because that would have been too obvious. This was where Summer and Byron came into play. Out of all the brothers, Byron was the weakest link. He had a hot head and was easily tempered which definitely made him react dangerously without ever thinking about the consequences. His second fault was also being in love with Summer ever since the day they met. If I could indirectly get close to him, I could make him betray the brotherhood. From what Summer had already told me, they all had a shared bank account that was fucking loaded with money. That was exactly what I needed to get out of this fucking hole that I had dug myself into but first I had to get past Tony which was no easy task. Summer and Byron were my pawns in this game of chess. Let the fucking games begin!

Chapter Nine:

Summer

"How was your day baby?" I asked as I massaged his shoulders.

"It was good. I signed a few new clients and took care of some contracts for the practice. How was yours?" he asked sighing.

"It was good. I had some 'me time' away from the boys and was able to relax on my day off. Things have been so tense between us lately and I know I'm partly the blame for that. I want us to get back to how we used to be," I said as I ran my hands down his chest.

"Yeah, I know baby. We've been like enemies lately but I miss the way we used to be too."

"I want to make it up to you," I said seductively as I stood in between his legs with nothing on but a silk robe that was tied at my waist.

"Oh really, how do you plan on doing that?" he asked as I dropped to my knees. It had been months since I'd given him head and I knew for a fact that he missed it because I was a nerd with the head game. I unbuckled his belt and unzipped his pants.

"First I'm going to start by swirling my tongue around the tip of your dick," I announced as I did just that. He instantly started moaning and I knew that I had him exactly where I wanted him.

"Damn, I have to meet with my brothers right now so let's just finish this when I get back home," he uttered between breaths. I wasn't hearing it though. I stopped teasing and deep throated him exactly the way he loved. He gripped the back of my head and thrusted his hips to go all in. I let him continue thrusting his dick into my mouth for a few strokes until I drew back to swirl my tongue around the tip again. I spit on his dick and looked up at him while stroking it with my hands.

"Now what meeting were you talking about again?" I asked rhetorically.

"Fuck that meeting," he moaned. I deep throated him again until he came inside of my mouth and I didn't miss a drop when he did.

After he caught his breath, I grabbed him by the hand and led him from the living room couch to our bedroom upstairs. I pushed him down on the bed and went to our stereo system to put on some slow music before dimming the lights. He watched and waited like a puppy waiting for a dog treat as I slowly untied my robe and let it drop to the floor. Although I had two beautiful boys, my body was still magnificent and he couldn't get enough of it. I was ready to ride him like a porn star and snatch his soul off of his body. I grabbed one of our pillows and placed it under his lower back. He asked me what the pillow was for and my response was for leverage both literally and figuratively. The pillow allowed me to ride him better by giving me more flexibility. I had already tried this little trick on the man I loved and it drove him crazy so I could only imagine how Byron was about to react. I straddled his lap in reverse cowgirl position slowly sliding his dick inside of me. We really hadn't had sex lately so I almost forgot how good he actually felt inside of me. We used to have the best sex and I think that was one of the things that kept us together for so long. I bounced my ass in his face while gripping his knees for balance. Surprisingly, I was enjoying myself and just as I was about to climax, he came. He only busted quick when he hadn't had sex so I knew he hadn't busted a nut in a while. Although I was happy that I still had him wrapped around my fingers, I was also frustrated because I was at my sexual peak and he just ruined it. I hid my frustration as he cuddled behind me and wrapped his arms around my waist. I thought to myself that this was the perfect time to get the joint bank account info that he had with his brothers.

"Baby, I have something on my mind that I've wanted to talk to you about," I said as I rubbed his arm.

"What's that?"

"I've been thinking about going into business for myself just like you."

"What type of business are we talking about?"

"I want to open a beauty parlor. Something like a one stop shop for women to get a massage, hair care, nail care, or just relax. What do you think?"

"I think it's a great idea but what about your job?"

"I'll leave it. That way I'm able to create my own schedule and spend more time with you and the boys." I was laying it on so thick that I deserved an Oscar award for this performance.

"If you're serious about this, put together a business plan and we'll go from there. Maybe this is what we need to mend our marriage." *Could he really be this blind? Could he not see that I'd been mentally and emotionally absent from this relationship?*

"I've already researched the average cost to start a business like this. I'd need approximately one hundred thousand dollars. Would we have to take out a loan for that?" I already knew the answer. I was just playing my role.

"Nah, I have that in the bank already. That's why I said if you're really serious we can make it happen ASAP."

"Don't you have to consult with your brothers first? I mean this is a big decision."

"I don't have to consult with anybody about my share of money," he stated with an attitude.

"Well I was just asking because I know everything must be presented to Tony before decisions are made." I was planting seeds of hate towards Tony and he was falling for it.

"You said that like Tony is my fucking daddy or some shit. Don't nobody tell me what to do. Remember that shit!" he spat.

"I'm sorry baby. Just forget that I even mentioned it. I know you're the boss." He didn't respond after that so my guess was that he was probably mentally replaying every encounter he previously had with Tony which successfully watered the seed I had just planted. The thing about it was all of the brothers were smart as hell but everyone knew that Tony was on a completely different level. He stayed ten steps ahead of everyone else. If Tony had a weakness, I wasn't aware of it. He seemed damn near untouchable, at least for now that is.

Chapter Ten:

Byron

Summer's words about Tony lingered in my mind. Why should I consult with him like he was my fucking boss? I started reminiscing and realized that Tony had always been the final decision maker throughout our lives. I couldn't recall a time when I didn't make a big decision without the council of Tony first. The more I realized this, the more upset I became. It seemed as if Summer respected him more than she respected me. Was I not the man worthy of her respect? What made Tony so damn special? These questions ran through my mind as I got dressed in an attempt to make it to our board plan meeting. I was already two hours late thanks to Summer but I couldn't pass up that opportunity. It had been months since we'd been this close.

When I finally made it to the warehouse, I used the watch Tevin had embedded with a special code to grant me access to our office. I bypassed the security gate and drove into the parking lot when I realized that everyone's car was still parked outside. That was extremely weird considering our board plan meetings usually lasted about an hour or two at the most. I parked my car and flashed my watch again to bypass the second security gate. I flashed my watch one last time in front of the code reader to enter our presidential conference room. I felt like a deer caught in headlights when everyone stopped talking and starred at me.

"Nice of you to finally join us," announced Tony.

"I was busy handling some business," I said as I took a seat at the table.

"Is that business more important than what's being discussed here?" he asked sarcastically.

"It depends on what's being discussed," I fired back.

"If you were here on time you would know that we have an issue. Where is your father-in-law?"

"Summer told me he's on vacation."

"And you believe that?" asked Tony.

"Why wouldn't I believe my wife?"

"Where is he vacationing?" he asked.

"Shit I don't know and I don't care. Why the fuck are you interrogating me all of a sudden?"

"Well lately, I've been noticing some unmarked cars around the warehouse and ironically Von goes on 'vacation'. Even a blind man could see what the fuck is going on here bro," he snapped.

"What the fuck does Von going on vacation got to do with this?" I was getting angrier by the minute.

"Come on B, you can't be that slow. I know you're smarter than this. Von is on 'vacation' around the same time unmarked cars start popping up all over the fucking place and I bet your wife did a fucking 360 too. You've become a liability B. I suggest you start watching your back."

"What the fuck do you mean my wife did a fucking 360?"

"What I mean is that bitch is probably back fucking and sucking you!"

"Don't call my wife no fucking bitch! I see you acting brand new since you been fucking that other bitch! You got a new piece of pussy and don't know how to act!" I yelled as I stood up from the table.

"Y'all calm down! It ain't even that serious!" yelled Tevin.

"It is that serious Tev! Shit is about to hit the fan and I bet his ass is blind as to what the fuck is about to go down! Wake the fuck up!" screamed Tony.

"Man fuck you and fuck all of you bitch ass niggas!" I yelled as I stormed out of the office. The only thing Tony said that was actually true was that shit was about to hit the fan. It just got real. I stormed out of the conference room as my adrenaline continued rushing throughout my body. If I didn't walk away now, me and Tony were about to throw hands that's for damn sure. I used my key to unlock the door of my truck as Tevin ran out of the warehouse calling for me to wait a second.

"Man, y'all tripping for no reason. You need to go back and clear the air because once you leave this building, anything could happen."

"Fuck that! I'm not going back in there so he can scold me like I'm a fucking kid! I'm a grown ass man! I don't have time for this shit!"

"So it's really fuck us huh?"

"Yeah I meant what the fuck I said! Me and Summer don't always see eye to eye but I won't let anyone disrespect my wife and the mother of my kids! I don't give a fuck who you are!" I announced as I hopped inside of my truck.

"You making a huge mistake B. Von don't have your back like we do," he announced with his hands in his pants pockets.

"That's funny! You really think Tony got your back huh? Tony only gives a fuck about Tony and the thing he loves most is to use and control us! I'm done being his bitch! Hopefully you are too," I said as I pulled off. I left behind the brothers I thought I knew with my tires screeching and rubber burning.

Chapter Eleven:

Antonio

"What the fuck just happened?" asked Julian.

"What happened is we just lost our brother. Summer's been all up in his fucking head. Since when does he come to meetings late? Any other time he can't wait to leave her and that house. I'll get to the bottom of this shit," I stated as I paced the floor.

"You know I got connects all throughout the police department. I'll ask around to see if Von has been on anyone's radar," said Julian.

"Yeah make sure you do that. We're talking about a man who loves being flashy and likes being seen. I'm sure he's been on somebody's fucking radar."

"I can't believe this shit is even happening," said Tevin.

"I can believe it. I saw this shit coming when Von started distancing himself from the organization. Unfortunately, B has been chosen as the weakest link and I can understand why. I love him but this shit is deeper than him. We all have to agree right here and now that Byron should no longer be in the loop when it comes to business matters. He can't be trusted. If you agree then say agree," I announced as I looked at everyone.

"I agree," said Jasper and Julian in unison. I looked at Tevin and waited for a response. I could tell he was hesitant.

"Are you sure this is the right move?" he asked.

"I'm sure Tev. This isn't personal. It's just business."

"I agree," he finally uttered.

"I know this is a hard decision but I think we can all agree that it's the smartest thing to do right now. Tev, I need you to revoke his access to the warehouse as well."

"I'm already doing that now," he claimed as he tampered with his business phone.

       I could feel a sudden change in the air as my brothers and I left the conference room without our brother B alongside us joking and talking shit. There was an energy shift between us as we felt the missing presence of Byron. We had never gone a single day without seeing or talking to each other so this wasn't an easy decision for any of us. However, business was business and we hadn't gotten this far by being soft. B had to be kept at arm's length until I could figure out what was really going on so bets believe I would have my eyes and ears on Summer. I know for a fact that she was behind this abrupt change in Byron. I suddenly felt a throbbing pain in my left temple. This stress was starting to become overbearing and too much for me to handle. All I wanted to do was relax so of course Angel swiftly crossed my mind. I found myself craving her presence so often to the point where I wanted her around me all day. I called her through my Bluetooth system in my car and waited for her to answer.

"Hello," she said.

"Hey baby. What are you doing right now?"

"I'm preparing for a therapy session I have in about twenty minutes. Is something wrong?" It was crazy how easily she could pick up on my emotions.

"I sure could use a night cap and some loving, and hopefully a back massage," I complained.

"Sounds like you had a long day. Once I finish up here I'll make my way over there and I will gladly give you some loving," she flirted.

"I like the sound of that. Just call me whenever you're on your way."

"Okay, I'll see you later babe," she announced as she hung up the phone.

Talking to her always calmed my spirit. There was just something about her energy that was serene and peaceful. Whenever she touched me, it was like each of my burdens and worries disappeared. When I made it home I was tempted to call Byron just to check on him and apologize for disrespecting his wife but the business side of me decided against it. I logged into the app that was connected to our joint bank account just to make sure everything added up. The doorbell suddenly rang the moment I was about to click on the dashboard to see the details of our account. I locked my phone and peeped through the peephole to see who was there. I smiled when I realized it was Angel. She wore a trench coat and had a bottle of wine in her hand. All I had on was a pair of basketball shorts and socks but I had a feeling I would be wearing nothing pretty soon. She was all over me as soon as I opened the door.

"I really missed you," she said as she kissed the side of my neck.

"I missed you too and I want to see what's underneath this trench coat," I said as I smacked her on her ass. She untied her trench coat and turned around in a circle as if she was modeling for me. She didn't have anything on underneath the coat.

"I figured why wear clothes when you were just going to rip them off anyways?" she chuckled.

"Yeah, you already know how I get down," I bragged.

"I figured we could take a bath together and I could give you a hot-oil massage to relax," she smirked.

"Yeah, I could use some relaxation."

We made our way to the bedroom and started running the bath water. I was overly excited for her to give me a massage and sooth away all the tension that had been bottling inside. We talked about how our day went as I laid between her legs while she drank wine. After we got out of the tub, she heated some massage oil and straddled my back to rub me down. I felt like the luckiest man on earth as she relaxed my body and my mind. When I was around her I felt like a normal person. I didn't have to pretend to be someone I was not. She accepted me for who I was. I had time to just relax instead of worrying about my next move to acquire money or about this sticky ass situation with Byron and Von. After she rubbed me down I wanted to get lost in her waters and dive as deep as I could but I also wanted to take my time before I took control. I wanted to make love to her like I'd never done with any other woman. I wanted to explore every inch of her body like never before. She laid on her back and invited me into ecstasy by spreading her legs apart. My first instinct was to slide my dick in but I was in the mood for some foreplay. I wanted to put her body on a pedestal because she had earned it. I started by kissing her neck and then licking and nibbling on her nipples as she whimpered and squirmed. I nestled in between her thighs and kissed around her pussy until I reached the middle to taste her other set of lips. I was amazed at her sweet flavor. If she didn't already know right then, I was pretty sure she'd find out soon that she has me wrapped around her manicured fingers. Although I was enjoying the foreplay, I'd much rather have her wetness wrapped all around me.

She still had her legs spread apart when I crawled in between them and slid into home base. This feeling never got old no matter how many times I felt it. It made me crave her even more. By the fourth stroke, I had already made up my mind that I wouldn't pull out this time. By the sound of her moans and nails clawing at my back, I knew she wouldn't object to it either so that's exactly what I did.

The next morning I woke up early to make breakfast again. I noticed she liked to sleep in on her off days but it wasn't like she needed to catch up on any beauty rest. She still looked beautiful to me even after she woke up with her hair matted. After I finished cooking, she showered and joined me at the kitchen table for breakfast. As I was eating my pancakes, I heard my phone vibrating on the kitchen counter. I normally turned it off whenever I was with Angel but considering what was going on with Von and Byron, I decided it would be smart for me to keep it on. When I answered it was Julian.

"Man, I've been calling you all fucking night! We have a problem!" he stated sternly.

"What's the issue?"

"Have you checked the joint account recently? If you haven't already, you gone be pissed when you do. Meet us at the office now! Jasper and Tevin are already there."

"I meant to check that shit last night but something came up. I'll be there in 20," I announced as I rushed to my bedroom to throw on some clothes.

After I hung up, I logged into our banking app and was shocked at the balance. Five hundred thousand dollars was missing which damn near emptied our savings account. This was our rainy day money for legal matters as well as our funds to get the fuck out of the drug game. We all took a percentage out of our monthly earnings and contributed to this account. We were the only ones who knew about this account and had access to it, or at least that was the arrangement. Although I had my own money, investments and separate accounts, the joint account was the money set aside specifically to step away from the drug game and start a new life. Adrenaline dashed through my veins as I rushed throughout the house gathering my shit before heading to the office. I was so angry that I completely forgot about Angel sitting at the kitchen table. I was pulling a hoodie over my head when she stood in the doorway.

"What's wrong Antonio?" she asked.

"I got some shit to handle. I need you to let yourself out," I spat.

"I don't appreciate the way you're talking to me and I damn sure don't like your tone," she fired back.

"I don't have time for this arguing shit Angel! I have bigger fucking problems than dealing with your fucking attitude right now so let yourself out like I said!" I yelled.

I was starting to lose control over my emotions which was something I never did in the past. I couldn't help but think that Angel had become a distraction. If she wasn't in my life I would have noticed this bullshit before the money was even yanked from our account. Now I had to play catch up which I despised. I watched her as she angrily gathered her clothes and quickly dressed. A part of me wanted to reach out to her and stop her from leaving but my pride wouldn't allow it. She grabbed her car keys and purse as she rushed out of the front door slamming it behind her without uttering a single word to me. When I finally made it outside and hopped in the car she was already gone. Although I felt like the biggest asshole for treating her that way, it still didn't stop me from handling my business. I burned rubber as I pulled off rushing to the warehouse.

"How the fuck did this happen?" I yelled as I burst into the conference room.

"There's no doubt in my fucking mind that this was an inside job. I checked the account a week ago and everything was there. What about y'all?" said Julian.

"Shit, it's been damn near two weeks since I checked. I know B or Tony usually checks the account so I can admit that I'd been slipping with that," said Jasper.

"Yeah it's been over a week for me too. I've been swamped at my company so it completely slipped my mind," announced Tevin. I thought back to yesterday when I was about to check the account. I had a nagging feeling that I should but of course I was distracted with Angel. *What if she was sent my way to distract me and throw me off my game? If she was then she was doing a damn good job.*

"Fuck! Fuck! Fuck! Has anyone talked to B since the last meeting?" I asked.

"Hell nah," everyone said in unison.

"Julian, have you heard anything about Von yet?" I was trying to keep calm amongst all of the bullshit.

"Not yet but I have a meeting with another detective tomorrow morning. Ironically, he's been looking for Von as well. I'll keep y'all posted on how that goes."

"Okay, sounds good. See if y'all can get in touch with Byron because I'm sure he won't reply to me. I feel like once we find out what the fuck Von is up to we'll get a clear picture of what's really going on."

Chapter Twelve:

Julian

I pulled inside the parking lot of the police station and got out of my vehicle. Once inside, I bypassed my colleagues and knocked on the door of a man who was now a well-respected seasoned detective. I'd never worked with him personally before but his record for successfully solving murder cases was remarkable. I waited a few moments after I knocked until I heard him ask me to come in. I entered and stood in front of his desk extending my hand out to formally introduce myself.

"Good morning sir, my name is Detective Julian..."

"I know exactly who you are Julian King. You were a police officer for two years before you took the psychological exam to become a detective. I also know that you passed that exam with flying colors. Your work ethic speaks for itself so no introduction is necessary here. Please, call me Greg," he announced as he stood and shook my hand. I felt honored that he respected my work ethic and already knew of me. I looked up to him ever since I was a kid.

"Nice to formally meet you Greg. Speaking of work ethics, your ability to solve practically every case you've encountered is impressive," I said as I took a seat in front of his desk.

"Thank you for your generous compliment but I feel as though bragging rights won't be earned until I'm able to put one of the biggest drug kingpins this city has ever seen behind bars where his ass belongs. Do you see those faces posted on my bulletin board over there?" he asked as he pointed to it.

"Yeah, I noticed it when I walked in."

"I'm glad you did because awareness of every small detail is important for what we do but that's beside the point. Those faces are thirteen individuals who have been murdered and I believe are linked to the hands of one person. That one person is Von Harris. This is a man who has instilled fear, drugs and murder into our communities for years now. This man has been untouchable but lately he's been sloppy. I promised the families of those individuals that I would bring them justice and I never break a promise."

"Wow, so you've been investigating Von for decades now?" I asked rhetorically. The irony of the situation was that Von had only been untouchable because he had my brothers and me on his team. If it weren't for us he would have been killed or locked up a long time ago. And now I had to investigate him as if I was never a part of his organization. How was that for irony?

"Yeah he's been elusive for years now, 27 to be exact. I'll be retiring in a few months but I must put him behind bars for this loaded case which is why I called you here. I need a pair of fresh eyes to review these cases. Would you like to assist me?"

"Absolutely! Nothing would make me happier than putting Von Harris behind bars," I announced with a smirk on my face.

"Sounds good. We're going to start bright and early tomorrow so come prepared to get your hands dirty," he announced as he stood up to shake mine again.

"I'm a man who is always prepared. I'll see you tomorrow morning." I stood and walked out of the office to leave the building. Once I made it to my car, I pulled out my cell phone to make a few calls. I had a number of friends who were FBI agents. Some of them were profilers and others were a part of the Narcotics Unit. I decided to call one of my buddies in the narcotics unit. He owed me a favor anyway I thought to myself as I waited for him to answer.

"What's up Jay! How have you been?"

"I've been good. I can't complain. How are things going in the federal world?"

"Man, shit has been hectic as usual but I can't thank you enough for helping a brother out with that informant. That info he provided helped close one of my toughest cases."

"No problem, I'm here to help whenever you need it but I sure could use a favor myself right now."

"Sure, what can I do for you?"

"I'm looking for any info you can get on Von Harris but this has to be off the record."

"Wow, the infamous Von Harris? I'm surprised this asshole hasn't been indicted yet but the last I heard he was on the run which I couldn't understand because his bank account had been frozen for weeks now. In order to get more info, I'll need to make a few phone calls and pull some strings. When I get something concrete, I'll contact you."

"Sounds good. The faster I can get some info the better. I appreciate this."

"I got you."

After I hung up the phone, I drove to Bryon's house to check on him but when I got there the house and driveway were both empty. I called my wife as I left B's house to see if she was busy at work. My baby also worked for the police department as a medical examiner. Our schedules were always busy but mine was a lot more unpredictable than hers so I would usually stop by her office throughout the day just to spend time with her. It had been awhile since we'd gone on a date so today I planned on having dinner with her. Just as I was pulling into the parking lot my phone rang. I answered without checking the caller ID.

"Hello."

"Hey, I just got the info that you wanted but I suggest we meet somewhere private because this information is sensitive."

"Just tell me when and where and I'll meet you there," I said as I waited for his instructions.

"I could use a cup of coffee so meet me at that café spot on Center Street in 20 minutes."

"Alright, I'll see you soon." I pulled into the parking lot of the café and walked inside. He was already seated with his cup of coffee waiting for me. He stood and shook my hand.

"I wish we could be meeting under better circumstances but here we are."

"Sounds like you have some bad news for me my friend," I announced as I took a seat.

"Yeah, you can say that. I can't give you the source of where I obtained this information because it's coming from one of my criminal informants but trust me when I say it's a reliable source."

"Okay, I'm listening. What do you have for me?"

"As I said earlier, Von being on the run has been confirmed by some inside sources. I checked his bank accounts and they were indeed still frozen. After making some phone calls, I realized that Von has some strong connections in the government and state offices. Man, this rabbit hole goes deeper than what I initially thought."

"So what exactly are you telling me here?"

"What I'm saying is someone in the mayor's office has been funding his run from the police. Some monetary transactions have been linked from the mayor's campaign fund directly to Von and his drug cartel. Once I'm able to pinpoint the source I'll contact you," he announced as he stood from the table.

"Thanks, I really do appreciate you for helping me with this case. I can't wait to put this bum behind bars."

"I agree. You should be hearing from me soon."

Chapter Thirteen:

Summer

I was shocked when Byron came home after his meeting with his brothers because the next morning he sprung a tropical getaway on me for just the two of us. He paid our nanny extra to babysit the boys and transport them to and from school while we went on an unexpected trip. It had been years since we'd been on vacation but I was more than ecstatic to get away from the city and soak up some sun on a tropical beach. We flew first class to St. Thomas and slept the majority of the flight. Since I didn't have time to pack for the trip, Byron gave me a stack to spend on myself while he handled some business he said he needed to take care of. He gave me instructions to meet him outside of our cabana once I was finished shopping and pampering myself. By the time I was through ripping and running, I needed to shower and change clothes. The weather was beautiful so I decided to wear a white strapless sundress that flowed in the breeze. I wore my hair up in a sleek ponytail and as I was putting on the finishing touches the doorbell rang. When I opened the door, I was shocked to see Byron because he was back earlier than he'd previously suggested. He had on a white button up shirt and khaki shorts with a fresh haircut. He looked good and smelled even better. It was then when I realized how much I'd always been attracted to him. He leaned in to kiss my cheek as he held a bouquet of red roses in his hands.

"You look as beautiful as the day I met you," he announced smiling.

"You look fine as wine," I bragged as I wrapped my hands around his abs. I felt old emotions I thought had died for him come back to life. *Am I still in love with my husband?*

"I have a special evening planned for us. I was just checking to see if you were ready."

"Yeah I'm ready I was just finishing up. What do you have planned?" I was curious.

"You'll see once we get to where we're going. I know you hate surprises but I think you'll enjoy the mystery of what I have planned," he said as he took my hand and walked me to the car waiting out front.

"Well at least tell me if I'm dressed appropriately for the occasion. I don't want to feel out of place babe," I whined.

"Trust me. You're perfect just the way you are." *Am I really perfect just the way I am? If only you knew that I am far from the girl you fell in love with that day in the restaurant. That little girl you loved is long gone. She's been replaced by a selfish, cheating bitch.*

I couldn't respond to him because I was deep in my own thoughts. How could he be so blind to who I was? How could he be blind to the type of woman I had become? Was love really this blinding? I looked at him and could see all of the love he had for me yet he was visionless when it came to my intentions with him. I really had his heart in my hands but the question was did I really want to break it? I was silent for the entire car ride because I was too conflicted with my emotions.

We finally pulled up to a beach just as the sun was setting and I must admit that the hues of pinks and purples in the sky paired with the warm breeze were breathtaking. As we approached the seashore we were met by an individual that announced he would be our tour guide for our sunset sail. I looked at Byron in amazement because he had put so much effort into making this trip a memorable, romantic getaway which made me feel even guiltier. He held my hand as we boarded the sail boat. Once we were comfortable, our tour guide pushed the boat away from the dock as the ocean carried us out into the horizon. I was lost in the sounds of the waves when Bryon intertwined his fingers with mine. I looked in his eyes and felt a rush of exhilaration run through my veins. It had been years since we shared this type of intimacy. I wished I could capture this moment to keep this memory and remember this feeling forever. If it were possible to freeze time, I most certainly would so I could relive this moment over and over again. I was starting to see a man who had finally matured. I could tell he was sick of constantly arguing even though I caused the majority of our arguments. I would start altercations with Byron on purpose just so I had a reason to leave and spend time with my other lover. Although I purposely pushed him away, I now doubted if that was even what I truly wanted. I had been so selfish lately that I never stopped to think about how my affairs with another man would affect my boys and our household. Was I mentally, emotionally and financially prepared for an ugly divorce or co-parenting with Byron? All of these thoughts raced through my mind as we continued holding hands. Suddenly, Byron's voice interrupted my daydream.

"Are you okay?" he asked with a look of concern.

"Yeah... yeah I'm fine. Why do you ask?"

"I ask because your palms are extremely sweaty and you have a really tight grip on my hand," he chuckled.

"Oh, I'm sorry. I was just daydreaming. This sunset is beautiful though. I wish the boys could see this too. I'm sure they would love it," I said as I cuddled closer to him.

"We can always plan another trip as a family. I just wanted some alone time with just the two of us," he announced as he starred at me. He leaned in and kissed my lips when I felt the sensations of arousal tingle within my groin. He cupped the side of my face with his hands which made me want to rip his clothes off. He pulled back with a huge grin on his face and gently placed my hand on his dick before leaning close to whisper in my ear.

"Do you feel that?" he asked as he bit my earlobe.

"I can't help but feel it," I said as I bit my lower lip.

We kissed and flirted with each other until we reached another dock with a table set on the white sands. As we approached the dock, I noticed lit candles decorated the table along with a bottle of wine, wine glasses and silver plates with matching lids. He smiled when he noticed my reaction to his romantic gestures. I was amazed and grateful for all of his efforts because I knew this wasn't an easy task to pull off. He helped me out of the boat once we docked as we began to walk hand and hand towards the table. He pulled out my chair allowing me to sit first before he went to take a seat across from me. Once he sat down, he reached over and grabbed my hands again.

"You enjoying yourself so far?" he asked as he caressed my hands.

"This is the best experience I've ever had babe."

"I love seeing you smile Summer. Seeing you happy, makes me happy." I felt guilt rise within me again.

"I love seeing you happy too baby."

"I know shit has been crazy lately with my brothers and with your dad. I'm not gone lie, this shit with my brothers is really starting to stress me out. We never fell off this hard before." When I looked him in his eyes, I could tell he missed his bond with his brothers which made me feel even worse.

"Y'all will get through this babe. Y'all probably just need some time away from each other," I said even though I knew it would take more than just time and space to repair the damage I had caused.

"Yeah you right baby. Enough of that though. I brought you here to have a good time, not to bring all of my problems here with us. I have another surprise for you too."

"You know I hate surprises but I'm curious to see what it is."

"I have to blindfold on you first." He stood up and took a blindfold out of his pocket and covered my eyes as he continued to speak.

"I didn't just bring you here to get away from my problems. This trip is more special than that. We've been through so much together. I've disrespected you, I've called you out of your name and I've mistreated you but one thing I've never done was cheat on you. I love you so much that it drives me crazy sometimes. I want to leave all of the pain we've caused each other in the past and move forward with a healthier relationship. Are you willing to let go of the past and embrace new beginnings with me? Take the blindfold off for me." I was surprised to see him on bended knee with a ring in his hands. He continued to speak as tears were already forming in my eyes.

"Baby, I want to renew our vows. I think this is long overdue. If you want another wedding, we can make that happen too. Whatever you want, I want to be the man to provide that for you. I love you and I can't imagine my life with any other woman. Will you marry me again?" he asked as he waited anxiously for my response. I had tears streaming down my cheeks which surprised me because I never considered myself to be an emotional woman.

"Yes! Yes! I will marry you a million times."

He stood up and embraced me as if he never wanted to let me go. We shared a kiss so passionate that I damn near wanted to skip dinner and rush to the bedroom but instead we sat back down, ate dinner and drank two bottles of wine. Everything was so perfect, I wished things could stay this way but my hopes were shattered as soon as my phone vibrated notifying me that I had received a text message from my dad. He had no clue of my whereabouts which I know concerned him since he practically always kept me right under his thumb. I glanced at his text that said he was going to call me at a specific time from an unknown number and for me not to miss his call. His text forced me to remember the role that he wanted me to play in order for his plans to go as scheduled but when I looked at Byron, I seen a man who worshiped the ground I walked on. As I got lost in my thoughts, I reflected on the nature of my relationship with my father. Somehow I always ended up being used by him for his own benefit. He never loved me the way a father should love his daughter. He was too selfish. He was only concerned about his reputation, his money and his cut throat image but when I looked at Byron, I seen a man who wanted to give me the sun, the moon and the stars. All he wanted to do was love me, build an empire with me and raise our boys together as a family and here I was plotting with my father to destroy all of that. How could I be so stupid? My father never treated me like family so why should I continue to protect him?

When we finished dinner, we sailed back to our cabana on the resort which was decorated with colorful patio furniture. We lounged around on the hammock and talked about future plans for our family. We even discussed getting marriage counseling to help us with our issues when we returned home. Once we finally retreated back to our bedroom, all I wanted to do was show him how much I loved and appreciated him. I felt the urge to give him all of me like I had never before. It had been awhile since I really made love to him without any ulterior motives. I had purchased some lingerie when I was shopping earlier that day because I seen a few pieces that I just couldn't pass up. I bought a black lace leotard that was sheer in all the right places with a matching black silk robe. After the day we'd just had, I figured tonight would be a good night to model it for him. I found myself so much happier in presence. Any other time, I couldn't wait to get away from him.

I ran a bubble bath for us while he took care of some paperwork that he claimed couldn't wait so I used this time to romanticize the environment and create a sensual ambiance. Tonight would be all about pleasing him. I went against my father wishes for the first time ever and turned off the ringer on my phone. I didn't want to interrupt my evening with my baby. I planned on giving him my full attention and effort because he deserved it and I didn't care who had a problem with it. I turned off the lights and lit a few candles while the wine chilled in a bucket of ice. I took my naked behind in the kitchen to grab the wine which immediately caught Byron's attention. He looked at me and smiled.

"You look mischievous like you're up to something."

"Maybe I am up to something. Just meet me in the bathroom as soon as you're done handling business so you can come and handle me next.

"Give me like five minutes baby and then I'll be in there."

"Okay," I said as I shimmied back to the bathroom.

I filled our wine glasses with some Italian red wine and turned on a playlist on my cell phone to set the mood. I stood in front of the mirror and gathered my hair into a bun when I heard the bathroom door creak. I smelled the scent of his cologne before he even approached me and wrapped his arms around my waist. I wrapped my arms around his neck while my body was on full display for him. It had been a long time since I was engulfed in love like this. My body craved his every touch and every being. I felt like such an idiot for even taking his love for granted so I decided from this day forth, I would never take it for granted again. I was sure my relationship with my father would suffer tremendously due to my loyalty to Byron and our family but they were my family and it was my job to protect it.

I turned around and started unbuttoning his shirt. I kissed his neck and chest while his shirt hit the floor. I knew where all of his spots were and took full advantage of that when I bit the side of his neck. I kissed down his chest and pulled down his shirts and briefs as I settled into a kneeling position to wrap my lips around his dick. I always got pleasure in teasing him and taking my time with easing my mouth down his shaft. When he moaned it was like music to my ears. It was verbal confirmation that I was pleasing him in every way possible. I honestly enjoyed giving him head and he enjoyed receiving it of course. In my opinion, it was like a power struggle that I loved because although I was on my knees which was typically a position of submission, I held all the power to break him down and bring him to his knees with the pleasure that I delivered to him. He palmed the back of my head as if it a basketball and verbally encouraged me to go faster so I did exactly as he requested.

I performed my favorite technique which was to give him head without using my hands to hold his dick. Instead, I used my hands to massage his chest, legs and balls because I wanted him to feel worshipped and surrounded with pleasure. He announced that he was about to come so I sped up the pace and anxiously waited for the grand finale. Unlike most women who stopped when a man busted I slowed down the pace tremendously continuing to swirl my tongue around the tip until he had the energy to pull out. When I looked up at him, I smiled at his reaction because it was validation that I had just snatched his soul away from his body. Knowing that I could have such an effect on him gave me satisfaction.

"You okay?" I asked as I stood from my kneeling position. I think he was literally stuck.

"Yeah, I'm good. I'm just weak at the knees at the moment," he chuckled.

"Well you can relax in this bath with me before the water gets cold," I announced as I grabbed him by the hand and took the lead.

I eased in the water first while he followed behind me and sat in between my legs. I handed him his glass of wine and then grabbed mine to take a few sips. I'd never felt so relaxed before now. I took the tips of my fingers and traced them along his broad shoulders and neck. He loved when I massaged his body and caressed him with my touch.

"No other woman can make me feel the way you do Summer. You're the only person to calm me like this. Everything with you just feels so right," he groaned as I massaged his shoulders.

"I feel the same way. Being with you just feels like home." I meant every word too. Even though I had another lover, I'd come to the conclusion that he could never replace the bond I had with Byron.

The water started getting cold so we decided to get out and dry off. The lights were off but the candles were still burning to provide a flickering light. He stood behind me and dried off my back with a towel as I stood in front of the bathroom mirror. He started kissing my neck as his hand eased between my thighs. He knew my body just as well as I knew his. When he bit the nape of my neck, he knew I couldn't help but shiver and moan. He eased his finger inside of me which was already as wet as the ocean so I hoped he was ready to dive in. He turned me away from the mirror, bent down to place my leg over his shoulder and buried his face in between my legs. He was always talented with his tongue and I'm sure tonight wouldn't be any different. The way he licked me was driving me crazy as I tried to grab anything I could get my hands on to keep my composure as he held me up by my hips. He stood and turned me back towards the mirror and slid inside of me in one quick motion. It's something about when the tip first slides in that drove me crazy and made me crave more. I bent over the sink and arched my back to give him more access and more leverage. His hands followed the dip in my back before he leaned back and gripped my hips. He had me open both literally and metaphorically and I must admit that I loved making love in front of the mirror because I was able to see all of the facial expressions that he tried to hide. Watching him enjoy every inch of me turned me on even more. I could tell he wanted to take his time but considering how good this pussy was I knew it was only a matter of time before he would lose control. I knew when he pulled my hair or wrapped his hand around my neck that he was going to bust a nut soon. I also knew that I would be joining him because I too was reaching my climax as my knees grew weaker.

"Go deeper," I demanded as I threw my head back. He responded to my request by doing just that as he bit the nape of my neck again. Surges of pleasure rushed throughout my body as I whimpered and moaned. He pulled out right after and decorated my lower back with his semen. He slouched over my body and kissed my neck again as we both tried to catch our breath. We looked at each other in the mirror and smirked like two teenagers who just had sex for the first time. We cleaned up the mess we made and retreated to the bed. We cuddled until he fell asleep in my embrace. I listened to him snore while I rubbed his neck and back.

I remembered that I never turned the ringer back on my cell phone so I eased out of Byron's embrace and grabbed my phone out of my purse. When I looked at it, I had several missed calls and five voicemails from an unknown number. I knew it was my dad but each voicemail I listened to was him just getting angrier and angrier about me not answering the phone. However, the last voicemail sent chills throughout my body which was ironic considering I was standing on a patio in the middle of the night surrounded by warm tropical weather. He coldly stated that he'd hate to see what would happen to me if I didn't follow through with his plan. It wasn't necessarily what he said but the way he said it that frightened me. There was no emotion as if I wasn't even a part of his bloodline. Was this a scare tactic to keep me in a state of fear or was he really capable of hurting me if I didn't abide by his wishes? I knew for a fact that he was a borderline psychopath so I wasn't trying to find out the answer to that question. I sent him a text message to his burner phone letting him know that everything was still going as planned. I also texted my lover to let him know that our fling was officially over. I blocked his number from ever calling me again and erased him from my list of contacts. I gazed at the stars in the sky and asked whoever was up there to watch over me and protect my family before heading back to bed with the only man who truly ever cared for me.

Chapter Fourteen:

Angel

How could he just kick me to the curb after having sex with me as if I was his personal prostitute whom he no longer needed to be serviced by? I'm sure my blood pressure was at an all-time high when I stormed out of his place. I slammed the door so hard that I tried to break the hinges off that motherfucker. How dare he treat me this way as if we hadn't shared something special just moments before our argument? I felt like he used me for his own selfish reasons and then discarded me like a recycled Kleenex. If there was one thing I hated the most, it was certainly feeling unappreciated and taken for granted. I had tears rolling down my cheeks as I made my way to Tori's house to vent and clear my mind. I wanted someone else's perspective simply because I knew I had a tendency of victimizing myself or even worst, conjuring up the worst case scenario and believing my own story. I continuously knocked on Tori's door until she opened it.

"How many times do I have to tell you to stop knocking on my damn door like the police? You are clearly not in the fucking suburbs Angel!" she nagged as she walked back to the living room.

"I'm having a midlife crisis and all you can nag about is my knocking? I guess you don't see that I'm an emotional fucking wreck right now," I said sarcastically.

"Are all rich people this fucking dramatic? You can miss me with the drama and just tell me all about this so called 'crisis' you're having."

"It's Antonio. We just had the biggest argument ever but it's the way he treated me that really pissed me off," I said as I grabbed a Kleenex from her coffee table and wiped my face.

"What did he do?"

"He basically kicked me out of his house after we had sex. I was supposed to stay the night again but he told me to let myself out after he got a phone call."

"Wow, sounds like he got another bitch or multiple bitches that he's juggling. I mean what did you really expect Angel? Did you really think he was going to be loyal to you when you two have only known each other for a hot second? I think you should cut your losses with him and move on to someone who's more of a 'clean-cut' type of guy." I was shocked at her response because this sounded nothing like her.

"Wow, this is a full 360 for you considering you seemed happy for me not too long ago."

"That was before you came in here crying. You've never dealt with the lifestyle of a criminal, let alone a man devoted to the drug game. I'm sure you can't handle the vices that come with that life Angel. Your prestigious upbringing won't be compatible with that." I was not feeling her tone or the vibe she was giving me right now. Even though Antonio pissed me off I still felt the need to defend him.

"Antonio isn't your typical corner boy on the block trying to make a dollar out of fifteen cents. He's a businessman. He's intelligent. He's an investor as well but you wouldn't know that because you don't know him the way I do."

"This man just kicked you out of his house after getting a call from God knows who and I bet you didn't see that coming so obviously you know him just as much as I do." I tilted my head to make sure I was talking to Tori and not my fucking dad because if I didn't know any better, I would've sworn he put her up to saying all of this.

"You know what, I think I should go before I say something I may regret," I announced as I stood to leave.

"Yeah, I think you should leave." I felt the energy of our bond shift from that of a sisterhood into enemies.

I walked to my car leaving more confused than I was before I even came to visit Tori. I sat in total silence as I tried to figure out everything that had just transpired in my life. Why is this happening to me? Everything seemed perfect just a while ago. I drove back to my place in a trance as my thoughts remained scattered. What if he does have other women he's dating? Did he really mean it when he said I was the only woman he wanted and trusted? Why pursue me if he already knew that he only wanted to play games and break my heart? I felt myself becoming overwhelmed with my emotions so much that I just broke down and cried on my living room sofa. I had never cried this intensely before. Not even when Trevor cheated on me. Why was I so emotional? I started crying harder whenever I thought about Antonio or read one of our old text messages that were filled with so much happiness when it suddenly hit me. The realization that I had never experienced a healthy, loving relationship with any of the men in my life sunk in. It seemed as though my relationship with my father was a reflection of how I handled intimacy with men. It was funny how I helped other people heal their childhood wounds using psychology but I neglected to heal my own. I guess that was the reason why Antonio's path crossed mine; so we could assist in each other's healing process.

As I cried, my mouth started feeling as if I was producing more saliva than normal. I felt the sudden urge to vomit so I rushed to the bathroom to puke in the toilet rather than all over the floor. I think everything I ate including my intestines had spilled over into the toilet bowel as I held my hair away from my face. I slowly stood and looked in the mirror. What the hell was going on with me? I washed my face and freshened up before grabbing my purse and heading to *Walgreens* for a pregnancy test. I rushed back home after grabbing the test and downed two bottles of water hoping to force myself to pee. I paced back and forth as I held the stick in one hand and read the instructions on the box in the other. I finally got the urge to pee so I sat on the toilet and urinated on the stick as instructed. Once I finished, I placed the cap back on the stick and anxiously waited for the results. My heart raced as two lines appeared on the stick indicating that I was indeed pregnant. I couldn't believe it! Were these results accurate? I waited until I needed to pee again so I could take the other test that came in the box. The results were exactly the same. I picked up my cell phone to call my doctor and set up an appointment. I was scared because I didn't know what to expect for this pregnancy. Would I encounter the same complications that my mother did? What if I ended up needing an emergency abortion or worst, what if this pregnancy was life threatening for me? How do I break the news to Antonio and how would he respond? We weren't even on speaking terms at the moment. He was clearly preoccupied with some other shit and now I had to add this to his plate.

I starred at his number in my phone and contemplated if I wanted to call him. Although I was mad at him, I did miss him and I wished we could get over this argument and get back to how we were before. Just as I was about to tap his name on my phone and call him, I received an incoming call from Tori. I was surprised she was even reaching out so soon after the way she had just acted at her place but I still answered. This wasn't the first time we had a disagreement and rekindled our friendship.

"Hello."

"Hey, I just wanted to say sorry for treating you the way I did earlier. Although you did ask me for my opinion, I feel like I mishandled the situation. You still mad?"

"Nah, I let that shit go once I left. I know you don't have filter Tori. That is nothing new," I chuckled.

"Good, I'm glad you said that because I'm outside of your house with a peace offering." I went to the window and peeked through the blinds. She was already on my porch so I opened the door for her.

"Damn you must be feeling really guilty," I laughed as I let her in.

"Nah, I just know I took my shit out on you because Shaun and I just had an argument right before you came over so I was already in a bitchy mood. I figured we could drink some wine and talk shit about the men in our lives," she giggled as she grabbed a pair of wine glasses from my kitchen cabinet. She handed me a glass of wine and started sipping hers. She looked at me and noticed that I sat my glass down on the table without drinking it.

"So I came all the way over here to drink with yo ass and you not going to have a drink with me?" she complained.

"I'm not really in a mood to drink."

"Come on Angel, one drink won't hurt. You'll drink with me any other time."

"Yeah that's true. I would have a drink with you but…" I paused and contemplated whether or not I should tell her I was pregnant considering how she just dogged Antonio a minute ago.

"Now you know I don't like that leading me on shit so 'but what'? If you got some juice you better spill it!" she demanded as she continued to sip her wine.

"I would tell you what's going on but I think it's better if I show you. I'll be right back." I went to my bathroom and grabbed the positive pregnancy tests out of the garbage next to the sink. She was sitting on the sofa when I returned.

"Girl, just tell me since you got me curious about whatever you about to tell me." I placed the tests on the living room table and told her to look at the results.

"I'm not touching that but I do see two lines on the window which means I'm going to be a Godmother! Oh my goodness! What did yo dad say about it because I'm sure it was nothing nice?"

"I haven't told him. I literally just found out maybe ten minutes before you called me."

"Did you tell Antonio yet?"

"Not yet. You're literally the only person who knows so far. I'm scared," I admitted.

"Yeah, I can understand why you're scared. How do you think Antonio is going to take the news?"

"I'm hoping he's going to be excited about it but I honestly can't even tell you how he would react. We're not even talking right now."

"Damn, that's fucked up."

"We'll get through this though. This ain't the first argument we've had so trust me when I say he knows he can't get enough of me. I'm not even worried. He ain't going anywhere," I said trying to convince myself more than Tori.

"Yeah, I can say the same thing for Shaun. I got his ass wrapped around my fingers too," she chuckled as she drank some more of her wine.

We chatted and watched TV as she continued drinking the bottle of wine. She stood up and said that she needed to use my bathroom and insisted that I don't have to stop the movie we were watching. I checked my phone for any missed calls or texts from Antonio while she was gone. I was devastated when I realized that I hadn't received any messages from him. We had never gone this long without communicating so I can admit that I felt a bit clingy and insecure. I read our old texts again and considered sending him a message but I didn't know what to say. I thought about sending him something full of sarcasm or anger but I simply asked him to stop by my place when he had some time for us to talk. Tori had been gone for a while so I called out to her to see if she was okay considering how tipsy she was.

"Yeah girl, I'm good I was just sending Shaun a text about how I felt. You know I sent his ass a paragraph," she stated.

"I hate to kick you out but I just got sleepy as hell so I'm about to go to bed. Thanks for coming over though. I really needed that," I said as I hugged her.

"You know I'm always here when you need me girl."

I locked my front door after letting her out and then went to my bedroom to undress and hop in the shower. I checked my phone like every two seconds because Antonio still hadn't responded. I couldn't help but feel some type of way about being ignored by the person I cared so much for. It was starting to bring a special kind of crazy out of me. I was literally fighting the urge to call him and cuss him the fuck out. I don't know if it was the fact that he was ignoring me or if it was my hormones from the pregnancy pushing me to be more irrational than normal; either way, my feelings were hurt and I was trying not to lash out on him. I stepped out of the shower and grabbed my towel to dry off. As I dried off my legs, I suddenly felt saliva building up in my mouth again like I had to vomit. I rushed to the toilet and puked until it felt like there was absolutely nothing left in my stomach to regurgitate. I didn't rush to get back up because after all of that, I still felt nauseous. I didn't have the energy to get back up anyways. All of a sudden, my doorbell rang as I laid there on the floor tired and a bit lightheaded. I didn't want my breath to smell like vomit so I quickly grabbed some toothpaste and my toothbrush to scrub my tongue and teeth. I swished some mouthwash around my mouth and then spit it back out into the sink. The doorbell rang again when I was just a few feet away from answering. I tied a knot in my towel to secure it around my breast before checking the peephole. To my surprise, it was actually Antonio. I know I asked him to come over but I was expecting him to call fist. Oh well, at this point it didn't even matter. I was just glad that he actually came over. I did a little victory dance at the door before opening it. I must have been right when I said he couldn't get enough of me. I calmed back down to gather my composure after dancing before opening the door to let him in.

"Hey, how have you been?" he asked as he embraced me with a hug.

"I've been good. What about you?" I asked as I closed the door behind him and locked it.

"I could be better. Honestly, I've been going through some shit but I wanted to come here and apologize for treating you the way I did. You really didn't deserve that. I hope you can accept my apology," he replied as he revealed the roses hiding behind his back.

"I accept your apology but don't ever talk to me like that again. What's been going on with you?" I asked as I placed the roses on my kitchen counter.

"I don't want to talk about that right now Angel. Can you respect that?" He looked so good right now, I thought to myself as I watched him take a seat on my sofa. He was wearing a black t-shirt and black jogging pants but when it came down to a man like Antonio, it didn't matter what he wore. I would still be fascinated with him.

"I can respect that. So what have you been up too since we haven't been spending any time together?" I asked as I sat across from him. I was probing to see if he'd been with any other women during our time apart.

"I've been handling some setbacks within my business. I haven't been kicking it with other bitches if that's what you're asking. I don't get down like that. When I say it's only you Angel, I mean that shit. I only want you." He looked me in my eyes as he spoke which lured me into him. He spoke with so much conviction and passion that I believed every word he was saying.

"That's not what I meant. I was just checking on you considering how you acted the last time we saw each other. I could tell something devastating must have happened but of course you wouldn't open up to me then like you're not opening up to me now," I couldn't tell him that the thought of him entertaining other chicks had in fact crossed my mind because I didn't want to show him that he had that effect on me. I didn't want to reveal my moment of insecurity but somehow he picked up on that anyways without me even telling him.

"I can't open up to you about certain things Angel. That's just the way it is for now. I don't want to involve you in this bullshit I got going on."

"So how do you expect for me to trust you when you can't even be vulnerable with me Antonio?"

"I can't answer that because vulnerability isn't a trait that I'm used to displaying. It isn't smart to be vulnerable in this type of business. You claim you can't trust me but let me ask you this, have I given you a reason to not trust me?" I took a moment to think about what he asked before responding.

"No you haven't."

"Okay then so what exactly is the problem?"

"I just want us to be honest and open with each other about everything."

"If you give me some time, I'll tell you everything that's going on but right now I can't do that. Have you been honest with me about everything?" he asked as he observed my behavior to his question.

"Yes, I've been honest with you." For some reason I couldn't tell him about me being pregnant. I felt like now wasn't the right time. He was already going through a lot of hurt and stress. He stood up and sat next to me on the sofa and grabbed my hand.

"I want to make something clear Angel. I don't know how to really express my emotions. Maybe it's because I've never met a woman who actually encouraged me to be vulnerable. Nor have I wanted to express my love for another woman but I love you. Being vulnerable isn't easy for me but I'll work on it if you work with me." *Did he just say what I think he said?*

"I love you too," I said as I hugged him. He kissed my lips and it felt like all of my previous anger I had towards him magically disappeared. As we were kissing, I suddenly felt the urge to vomit coming up so I ran to the bathroom and puked in the toilet. Antonio rushed in after me and held back my hair.

"Damn baby, what's wrong? Are you okay?"

"I'm good. It must have been something I ate. I think I have food poisoning." I uttered in between hurling. When it finally stopped, he helped me to my feet.

"What did you eat?" he asked as he rubbed my back.

"I had some soup the other day and I think it had some meat in it," I continued to lie.

"I was just dropping by because I have some business to handle early tomorrow morning but if you want me to stay the night and take care of you I can."

"If you could stay that would be great. I haven't been feeling well all day."

"Come here girl," he chuckled as he picked me up.

"Where are you taking me?" I laughed.

"I'm taking you to the bedroom. You need to lie down and relax."

He laid me down on my bed and turned on the TV before going to the store to buy some ginger ale and ice cream in an attempt to make me feel better. When he came back, he took off his clothes and hopped in bed cuddling up behind me. I wanted to have sex so bad but I was still nauseous and I might have to vomit again. Vomiting during sex was not sexy whatsoever so I opted out this time. I definitely missed his presence and missed cuddling with him. We cuddled and talked until I eventually drifted off to asleep. Things couldn't have been more perfect between us.

The next morning I woke up early to head to my doctor's appointment. I wanted to double-check and see if these home pregnancy tests were accurate. If they were, then I would tell Antonio so we could start the journey of preparing for a healthy pregnancy. Antonio was up bright and early right along with me preparing to head to his meeting but before leaving, he wanted to make sure I ate some breakfast. Although the breakfast he cooked was good, I only nibbled on it because I felt too queasy to eat anything. My mind was too preoccupied with hiding this from him for now. I didn't tell him about the appointment because I wanted to be sure that I was pregnant and of course I was waiting for his life to be less hectic before breaking the news to him. I was grateful that my doctor was able to squeeze me into her schedule. She said it must have been my lucky day since she was actually able to see me on such short notice. If someone hadn't cancelled their appointment, I wouldn't have been so fortunate. I waited in line at my doctor's office to check in with the receptionist. Once I finally made it to the front, I took out my insurance card and photo I.D.

"Good morning, I have an 8 o'clock appointment with Amanda," I announced as I handed her my cards.

"I'm sorry but Amanda isn't in today due to a family emergency. Would you like to reschedule your appointment for another day?" I was instantly irritated. Normally, things like this wouldn't bother me but my emotions and hormones were all out of whack so I snapped at her.

"Someone in the office could have contacted me and informed me before I came all the way over here. Do you realize I had to take off work to be here for this appointment which means I'm losing money at this very second and I wasted my fucking gas!" I don't know why I was complaining about gas money when money had never been an issue for me. The fact that I already felt like shit just encouraged me to bitch at her even though she was just the messenger.

"Again, I do apologize. I can check the appointment book to see if there's another doctor available right now if you're open to seeing someone other than your PCP," she suggested.

"I would like that. I didn't come here for nothing so please see if someone is available," I spoke more calmly than before.

"Okay, give me a moment," she replied as she focused her attention on her computer screen. She typed loudly for a few seconds and then responded.

"Okay, I found a doctor who has an opening but it's a male doctor. Are you comfortable with that?"

"Yes, I'm comfortable with it."

"Sounds good. He's available right now so I will call him and let him know you're waiting. In the meantime, you can have a seat in the waiting area until a nurse calls you back."

"Thank you. I truly appreciate it."

"No problem," she announced as she picked up the phone.

I took a seat and pulled out my cell phone to check for any missed calls or texts. I had a missed call from my dad but I decided now was not the time to deal with him and his shenanigans so I replied to a few work related emails instead before the nurse called my name. When I made it to the back area, she took my weight and vitals before placing me in a room. I sat on the chair as she asked me a few preliminary questions and then informed me that my doctor would be in shortly. After a few moments, there was a knock at the door. The doctor was tall and dark-skinned with grey hair and grey eyes. He looked good for his age and I couldn't help but think that he looked familiar.

"Good morning Ms. Angel. How are you on this lovely morning?" he asked as he stood in front of me.

"I'm not feeling too well but I'm okay considering the circumstances."

"So what brings you in today?"

"I want to confirm whether or not I'm pregnant. I took two home pregnancy tests but I want to be sure since I've never been pregnant before."

"Okay, I want you to go to the bathroom on the left at the end of the hall. There's a cup there with your name on it. Once you're done with the cup, place it inside the metal cabinet in the bathroom and we'll go from there," he stated. I did as instructed and urinated inside of the cup. Once I was through, I placed it inside of the cabinet and washed my hands before heading back to my assigned room to wait for the doctor.

"So I ran the urine sample and you are indeed pregnant. I'm not sure how far along you are since I don't have your file but I'm going to estimate and say that you're approximately 1-2 weeks pregnant considering you're not showing at all. When was your last period?" he asked as he sat at the computer. I gave him the date and he entered it into the database.

"I knew it! You're two weeks pregnant. You can break the news to the lucky guy because I'm sure a woman like you should already be taken," he flirted.

"Yeah, he's the love of my life. I can't wait to tell him the good news! He actually favors you a lot in the looks department." I smiled as I thought about him.

"Really? I don't hear that too often because I'm a rare looking guy. What's his name if you don't mind me asking?" he inquired as he brought his attention to me.

"His name is Antonio. He has beautiful grey eyes too so I'm hoping our child will inherit them as well," I bragged. I noticed the doctor's demeanor abruptly changed from happy to concerned.

"Well Antonio is certainly a lucky man. I would love to continue being your doctor throughout the duration of your pregnancy if that's okay with you?" I actually didn't have a problem with that since he reminded me a lot of Antonio. Plus, he made me feel welcome as a new patient of his.

"Sure, I would love that. So what is the next step? I'm new to this."

"I'll prescribe some prenatal vitamins for you to consume daily and you can go ahead and schedule your next appointment with the receptionist. That's when we'll check for the fetus's heartbeat. I'm looking forward to working with both of you," he smiled.

"Thank you for seeing me on such a short notice. I must have pregnancy brain because I don't remember your name."

"My name is Kenneth but you can call me Kenny," he announced as he reached out to shake my hand.

"Enjoy the rest of your day Kenny," I said as I grabbed my purse and exited the room. I was excited more than ever but now I just had to find the right moment to tell Antonio the good news.

I called Tori when I got back to my car and told her exactly what the doctor said. Although I was excited, I was also scared because I still didn't know how to break the news to Antonio. In his mind, he thought I was sick with food poisoning. He had no clue I was actually carrying his seed. Being that he was so good at picking up on every little detail worried me because I was sure it was only a matter of time before he realized that I was pregnant. He had already mentioned that I was "glowing" more than usual so it wouldn't surprise me if before long he would put two and two together. I called Tori because I needed advice with this particular situation.

"I was completely lost about how to tell Antonio. Should I even tell him right now? He already had so much going on," I rationalized.

"Yeah but eventually you'll have to tell him Angel. It'll be best if you just tell him now rather than later and he'll definitely be pissed if he figures it out on his own."

"Yeah you have a point but I don't even know the words to say to him which is funny because I'm never at a loss for words."

"You should try rehearsing what you want to say so that you'll know exactly how you're going to say it."

"That sounds like a good idea. I can role play with you right now," I chuckled.

"Nah, I think it'll be best if you practice with Shaun so you can have a male's perspective and genuine response. We're actually on our way to a Jamaican restaurant to grab something to eat. You can meet us here if you like."

"That sounds good actually. I'll see y'all soon."

I spotted them sitting in the front window as soon as I pulled up. I hugged Tori once I made it inside and took a seat across from Shaun. They already had their food when I arrived. I was going to call over the waiter for him to take my order but the smell of the food alone made me nauseous. Tori said she had a phone call to make so she stepped out of the restaurant to do so. As soon as she left, Shaun asked me a couple of questions about my pregnancy and started role playing with me as if he were Antonio. I think he took it a little overboard when he reached across the table to hold my hands especially since Tori wasn't around but I admit that role playing with him did put my nerves at ease. I finally felt comfortable enough to share this news with Antonio. I stood up and hugged Shaun to thank him for helping me out. I also hugged Tori goodbye once I stepped outside since she was still on the phone when I left.

Chapter Fifteen:

Von

Summer must have thought I was fucking stupid or something. She suddenly tries to go missing in action without realizing that I had eyes and ears every fucking where. I didn't need to be in the same town as her to know what the fuck was going on. Nevertheless, I noticed everything. I knew she was changing. She was no longer apart of the agenda which is exactly why I had a plan B already in place just in case she decided to switch up on me. She was my only child so I expected her to be a part of my organization but I was also aware that blood wasn't always thicker than water. I hadn't survived in this game so long for nothing. I was well aware that anyone could change up on you at any given moment but sadly enough, I expected more loyalty from my own seed. I was sitting low in the front seat of my car behind tinted windows rolling a blunt. My nerves had been so shot lately that I started smoking daily just to ease my mind. I pulled out my burner phone and made a phone call.

"Hello," he answered.

"Yo, have you heard from Summer yet?"

"Not since she sent me that text the other night. I called her several times and each time it went straight to voicemail. I did a little drive-by by her house and it looked like no one was home."

"What the fuck man! I thought you were handling business? You're supposed to be the player of the fucking century yet she's still stuck on Byron's bitch ass! I paid you to do one job and you fucked that up!"

"Relax. All isn't lost yet my friend. Just give me a week and I bet I'll have the info that you paid for. She has feelings for me. Just give me time to play on her emotions," he said persuasively.

"You got seven days to make a fucking miracle happen and I mean only seven days! I'm running out of time, money and patience! You contact me as soon as you get something. You hear me?" I snapped.

"Seven days is all I need. I don't get paid top dollar for nothing. I'll touch base with you soon," he bragged. I slapped the flip phone shut and rubbed my temples. This shit was becoming too stressful. I'd been trying to get my hands on that account information for the past few months and I was counting on this nigga to make it happen; now my plan was backfiring. My burner phone rang as I exhaled the smoke. I already knew who it was since only one other person has this number.

"Hello."

"I thought everything was going as planned. What the fuck happened? The election is coming up soon and I'll be damned if I don't get reelected because of all the fucking drug trafficking problems in the city! We had an agreement but it looks as if you can't handle your end of the deal!" he yelled.

"Aye, I don't know who you think you talking to but when you come to me you come correct! Don't worry about my end of the deal because shit is getting handled. I had a little setback but the comeback is gone be even better so get the fuck off my back and give me time to hand you this nigga head on a platter. Shit like this takes time!" I was getting tired of this old motherfucker hounding me like I didn't already have enough shit going on. I didn't answer to any fucking body!

"How much time you think you need? I must stress that I'm on a strict time frame. I have to let the people know that something is being done about the city's drug problem. What better way to show them than by putting away the biggest king pin in this city?"

"Listen, Tony isn't your typical corner boy. This motherfucker is literally the smartest fucking person I know so he doesn't move like every other drug dealer. This nigga doesn't trust people so you have no idea how hard it's going to be to catch his ass slipping? He doesn't leave paper trails. He doesn't make mistakes and everyone respects him so much that they refuse to turn on his ass so I have to literally make some shit happen! Give me at least two weeks."

"Okay, you have two weeks but if he isn't in police custody by that time then my protection for you expires and you'll be left to fend for yourself," he claimed before hanging up in my face. If his old ass wasn't a government official, I would've had his disrespectful ass handled a long time ago. As much as I hated to admit it, I needed his protection from the police. I'd already been interrogated on several occasions and with his help they could never make the charges stick. The prosecution would somehow "lose" critical and incriminating evidence or witnesses suddenly decided not to testify against me. I didn't know what type of power this motherfucker had but I'd be damned if I didn't keep him in my pocket.

Chapter Sixteen:

Greg

"It's been a long time since I've heard from you. I know we've both been busy lately but how you been?" I said to Kenny as I stood up from the table and hugged him. We'd been good friends since middle school. Good friendships like that were hard to come by nowadays.

"Man, I don't even know where to begin. The other day, I met my son's significant other. It just so happened by chance. I saw her face quite often at our hospital and I would have never thought in a million years that she would be my son's significant other. More importantly, she's carrying my soon to be grandchild," he smiled.

"So I guess this means you can no longer hide in the shadows of Antonio's life anymore. You know it's never too late to establish a relationship with him right? He deserves to know who you really are Kenny."

"I know, I know. It's like every time I get the balls to tell him the truth I take the cowardly way out and remain silent but now that I've met his woman and realized I have a grandchild on the way, it put things into perspective. I have to tell him the truth now."

"Yeah, there are a lot of things we should tell him that he doesn't know about. Although Antonio is playing with fire doing what he's doing, I must say that I have nothing but respect for him. He has never used the drug game to kill anyone for respect. He earned his respect with his intellect and the love he's shown to those in and out of his organization. That's exactly why I've always been torn between what's legally wrong and what's morally right. The fact that I've witnessed his limited resources and everything he endured as a child played a huge role for me deciding to help you protect him."

"I know and you know your help is much appreciated my friend. I know he's more than capable of taking care of himself but I'll be damn if I let anything happen to my boy."

"So when are you going to tell him the truth and most importantly, when are you going to let him know that we're responsible for draining their joint account?" I pulled some strings with one of my friends at the police department to hack their savings account and take the money. Based off what Kenney said, the money was in the process of being handed over to Von Harris. I'll be damned if he took that money and used it to flee the city. Plus, I know Tony wants to get out of the drug game so we just put the money up for safe keeping.

"I plan on telling him everything when he and his lady come to their next doctor's appointment. When he takes one look at me, I'm sure he'll know exactly who I am anyway."

"Yeah, you couldn't deny him as your son even if you wanted to," I laughed as I sipped my coffee.

"Trust me, I already know. I just wish Angela could be here to witness just how gifted and amazing our son turned out to be." Kenny had never gotten over Angela's death and he still felt responsible no matter how many times I told him otherwise. I could only sympathize with him because I didn't know what it was like to endure everything he'd been through.

"Eventually you have to let that pain go my friend. You've been carrying this for decades now. Aren't you tired of carrying the hurt with you everywhere you go?"

"It's always easier said than done Greg. All I can think about is what if I had answered the phone that night when she called? I'm sure if I had answered she would still be here so I am responsible for her death and Antonio being raised by shitty ass human beings."

"You may feel responsible because that's the way your brain is rationalizing the pain you've experienced but at the end of the day, you didn't kill Angela and you didn't put your son in foster care. She made those decisions Kenny, not you."

"I guess you have a point when you put it that way."

"I know I do but the good thing is now you have a second chance to make things right with your son and your grandchild. You have to start living in the present and let go of the past because you can't change it."

"Yeah, you're right. Thanks for always being there for me man."

"You're my brother from another mother. You know I always got your back. Finally, I'm excited to formally meet Antonio without hiding in the background. I've been working with his brother Julian just to keep a close eye on everything and everyone. He doesn't even recognize who I am but I know exactly who he is. Those boys in raggedy clothes turned into grown, successful black men so who am I to tear down what they've built when I know where they come from?"

"And I thank you for that because you've been walking a thin line by helping me protect my son and his brothers but like you said, it's a battle between what's legally wrong and what's morally right. I can't thank you enough for covering up what happened with Antonio and his foster mother."

"I told you we never have to bring that up again and you don't have to thank me for having loyalty to a good friend. Speaking of work, I have to go to the Mayor's office to meet with him."

"Why are you meeting with that scrub? I've never liked that dude. Every move he makes is for the cameras. He couldn't care any less about actually being a leader for the people."

"I can't stand his ass either but the chief claims he's been requesting to meet with me for quite some time now. I've been avoiding the meeting but the chief is basically forcing my hand on this one. You know how that politics shit goes," I said I stood from the table.

"Yeah trust me, I know how that shit works. I'll let you know how it goes with Antonio when I see him. Wish me luck."

"You don't need luck. I have faith in you. I'll see you soon."

I left the coffee shop and made my way to the mayor's office. My chief made sure to keep me in the dark about why the mayor, of all people, even wanted to meet with me. In an attempt to back out, I sure as hell bombarded chief with a thousand questions. I was desperately looking for an excuse to not attend this meeting. When I made it to the lobby, the mayor's receptionist checked me in and notified him that I had arrived. He smiled his usual fake smile and led me into his office. I admired the expensive décor as he poured himself a drink and I took a seat on his leather couch.

"Would you care for a drink?" he asked.

"No thank you. Let's just get to the point. Why do you keep requesting to meet with me? Why am I here?"

"Wow, hasty aren't we? I just thought you of all people could use a drink considering the heavy work load you have on your plate."

"Please spare me the drama and save it for the movies. What do you want?" He was testing my patience.

"Are you still investigating Von Harris as a suspect for those unsolved murder cases?"

"That's not any of your business to be honest with you." *I could see where this was headed.*

"You must be misinformed detective. You see, I'm the mayor of this city which means you being an employee of the police department that I am in charge of as a legislative enforcer means it is MY business." I looked at him as if he was the scum on the bottom of my shoe.

"The information in this case is sensitive and confidential but I will say that yes, he is a suspect until I rule him out."

"You do realize that I have the power to reassign the case to someone else? Perhaps someone who's more qualified to solve this case because this doesn't look good for the city and most importantly, it doesn't look good for me as a Mayor. I want you to not just focus on Harris. You need to look for other suspects because I'm sure there's more than one perpetrator in this case. If you have an issue with looking into other suspects, you will be permanently removed from the case. Understood?" I looked at him with so much hate and I didn't even care to disguise my disdain for him.

"I understand," I announced as I stood to leave. *I understood that he was a crooked ass mayor and I planned on making sure he got exactly what was coming to him. That applied to both him and Von Harris since he wanted to protect that devil.*

Chapter Seventeen:

Antonio

After leaving Angel's house the next morning, I went to Tevin's company to meet with him. I still hadn't figured out who was responsible for taking the money out of our account and it was really starting to piss me off. There had never been a riddle that I couldn't figure out. I really wanted to stay with Angel and make sure she was feeling better but this was something I couldn't postpone. Tevin was also trying to figure out what happened to our money but he had been met with the same outcome. We were both confused. He called me and told me that he had something to show me so here I was in his office.

"You know I don't like not being able to figure this hacking shit out so I've been working on this every chance I can get. I wanted more insight before I came to you but this shit is crazier than I thought."

"What did you find out?" I asked as I stood over his shoulder with both of us glaring at his computer screen.

"Whoever hacked into our savings account knew exactly what they were doing. They must have been a fucking professional. They bypassed the electronic firewall that our bank had in place to protect our personal information and they used a malware program to steal our login."

"Come on Tev speak English and break it down in simple terms for me," I don't understand all of this hacking terminology that he is used to using on a daily basis. It sounds like gibberish to me at this point.

"So simply put, they bypassed the firewall to gain access to our bank's system and then used keystroke logging which is a program that records login I.D's. Once they had our login information, they accessed our account and drained out all the money. Now that I've figured out how it was done, I can back track and pinpoint who did it. Every device has a numerical fingerprint that's connected to an internet protocol which means I can track their internet activity and pinpoint their exact location." I looked at my brother in amazement because no one could hold a candle to him when it came down to this computer programing and hacking shit. I could see why the National Security Agency in the U.S. Intelligence Group had been trying to head hunt him. He declined because he simply preferred to be his own boss and run his own company.

"You are the fucking man boy!" I yelled as I shook him by the shoulders.

"I just need another day or two to find their IP address and then I'll really be the fucking man!" he claimed as we bumped fists.

"Call me when you figure that shit out. I gotta go bust another move so I'm out."

Alright, I got you bro."

After I left Tevin's office, I went to the gym to relieve some stress and tension that had been building up since this shit happened. When I made it home, I pulled into my driveway and hopped out of my truck. As I approached my front door, I could see an unmarked manila envelope on my doormat. I looked around to observe my surroundings but I didn't see anything out of the ordinary. I picked it up and went inside the house. I placed it on the kitchen counter and hopped in the shower so I could put on some lounging clothes. I went back to the kitchen and starred at the envelope. I had a feeling that whatever was inside would somehow change me as a man.

I took a deep breath before I pulled out its contents and I couldn't believe my eyes. Inside the envelope were photographs of Angel on a date with some dude who I had never seen before. There were different shots and angles of them holding hands, hugging and staring at each other like she was madly in love with this nigga. I felt a sense of rage rise within me like never before. I never loved anyone the way I loved Angel so to see her with another nigga right after me telling her that I loved her infuriated me. I knew I had anger issues and I was trying to deal with them and de-stress without lashing out at others but this shit had unleashed an entirely new level of rage that I'm sure no one would care to see. If I had a punching bag, I would've been fucking it up but instead I relatively punched a hole in the wall. Had she been playing me for a fool this whole fucking time? Here I was trying to be vulnerable and honest about myself and everything I had gone through when I really shouldn't have. This was exactly why I don't trust women because once you fall in love with them they had the power to break you. How could I have been so blind to this bullshit?

I paced back and forth across the living room floor debating with myself which calmed me down a tad bit but I was still beyond angry. I didn't call her or any of my brothers because I knew that if I did, I'd definitely explode. I took a few deep breaths and wiped away the tears that were streaming down my face. I wanted to handle this like a man and confront her but I needed to be calm in order to do so. I went to my closet, threw on a black hoodie and headed over to her house. I sped the entire way there while gripping the steering wheel so hard that the veins in my hands began to protrude. I whipped into her driveway so fast that I barely put my truck in park before hopping out. I needed to calm down so I took a few more deep breaths before ringing the doorbell. Everything felt like it was moving in slow motion as I waited for her to answer the door. What if that nigga was here right now? Lord I hope he isn't because I don't want to catch a case tonight or worst, I wasn't trying to kill another person. When she opened the door she had on one of my t-shirts with her hair pulled back in a sloppy bun. Her skin was glowing and she was as beautiful as the day I'd first met her but I was still on a fucking mission to get some answers from her. I needed to know if she was really rocking with me because she loved me or did she have a secret agenda against me? I played it cool and kept my cards close so she wouldn't notice that I was angry. It took all of my might to play dumb.

"Hey babe, I've missed you so much. I feel like I haven't seen you in forever!" She claimed as she hugged me. If I said her touch and her perfume didn't turn me on I'd be lying. I hated that she had this effect on me.

"I know. I've been busy tying up some loose ends. Are you feeling any better?" I asked as I locked the door behind me. As I looked at her, I could tell she was about to vomit again. She held up one finger for me to wait a minute as she ran to the bathroom. I heard her vomiting seconds later. When I sat down on the couch she called out for me.

"Babe can you please grab me another t-shirt out of my dresser? I puked all over this one." she explained.

"Hold on," I said as I went to her bedroom to look in the dressers. I pulled out one dresser drawer that was filled with bras and panties. I checked another one that had clothes in it so I started searching for a large t-shirt. At the bottom of the drawer was a tan file folder with a small picture of me attached to the top, left corner. I flipped it open and started reading its contents. The more I continued reading the file, the angrier I became. The file had my home address, the address to our warehouse, other photos of me that were clearly taken without my knowledge, and pictures of all the vehicles I owned. This was an investigation file! Man did she have me fooled! I never would have expected this, especially from her out of all people. I grabbed my own file from my hoodie and pulled out the pictures of her and this unknown nigga. I waited for her on her living room couch. By the time joined me in the living room I was already filled with rage, my heart was breaking, and I had tears threating to leave my eyes. How could she deceive me like this?

"I have good news to tell you," she claimed as I heard her turn off the water in the bathroom. I didn't respond.

"Did you hear me?" she asked as she stood in front of me in the living room.

"It's funny that you have good news because I have some news for yo ass too. What the fuck is this bullshit?" I yelled as I stood up from the couch and dropped the files on her coffee table. She looked confused as she picked them up and sorted through them. She was such a great actress that she deserved an award for this performance.

"Wait, how did you get these photos? I literally just had this meeting yesterday. I don't understand what's going on," she claimed as she continued to lie.

"Oh, you don't understand huh? Let me clarify some shit for you then. This bullshit right here is you fucking cheating on me and this other bullshit is you playing me like a fucking fool! I trusted you Angel! I fucking love you and this is how you betray me? So what's next? You plan on turning me in to the fucking police? Is that why you've been fucking investigating me? You were playing me this whole fucking time!" I yelled as I paced back and forth. I could feel myself losing control to the point where I was going to go off the edge.

"I'm not cheating on you Antonio! I would never cheat on you! This guy in the picture is my best friend's boyfriend! How did you even get this shit?" she yelled back at me.

"I don't believe that shit! So where's your best friend in this picture? Would she be cool with her nigga hugging all over you? Don't ever fucking call me! I never want to see your fucking face again! I'm done with you and this fucking relationship!" I yelled as she tried to explain. I punched a hole in the wall of the hallway leading to the front door. I figured it would be best to hit the wall then to put my hands on her. That's how furious I felt. I rushed out the front door and slammed it. When I got inside my truck, I broke down and cried. I was filled with anger, love, hate and confusion all because I truly loved her and she played me. I started up the truck when she came outside to try and stop me from leaving. I quickly reversed and sped off leaving her crying in the middle of the driveway.

Chapter Eighteen:

Angel

I couldn't believe what just happened. I was in shock that Antonio was even capable of treating me with such disdain and he had the audacity to think I actually deceived him in such a way. I sobbed uncontrollably as I made my way back inside the house. The smell of his cologne still lingered in my living room. I was already an emotional wreck thanks to this pregnancy that had been kicking my ass and now I had to deal with him breaking up with me? I never even had the chance to tell him I was pregnant. I wanted to call Tori and vent to her but my instinct told me to hold off on that. When I did finally calm down, I noticed that he left the files on the table. I was so concerned about the photos with Tori's boyfriend Shaun that I didn't really observe the other file folder. Suddenly, it dawned on me that it was the file my father showed me the day we had brunch and he threatened me to not date Antonio. Wait, how the hell did my father's file even end up in Antonio's hands? I don't remember seeing Antonio carrying a file with him when he arrived so he must have found it when I asked him to grab me another t-shirt. I didn't remember keeping the file when my father showed it to me so how the hell did it end up in my house and furthermore, how did it get in my dresser?

I observed the photos again and realized they were taken when Tori stepped out of the restaurant to "ironically" make an important phone call. I also remembered that this was exactly when Shaun started touching me inappropriately. I didn't believe in coincidences. This shit was definitely orchestrated! I thought about all of my previous interactions with Tori ever since I started dating Antonio. Initially she was happy for me but then she started switching up on me. That day when she brought over the bottle of wine as a peace offering quickly came back to mind. Was she really texting Shaun when she disappeared to the bathroom for a couple of minutes or was she planting that fucking file in my bedroom? The same day she spoke negatively about Antonio, she sounded exactly like my father. All of the slick comments and shade she'd been throwing suddenly made me realize just how envious she truly was. All of the dots began to connect but one question still remained unanswered... why would she do this to me?

I had my follow up appointment with my new doctor the next day and despite of all of the crazy shit happening in my life, I was still excited to hear my baby's heartbeat for the first time. I tried calling Antonio several times but his phone went straight to voicemail. I basically ended up crying myself to sleep that night. The next morning, I dragged myself out of bed and threw on some clothes to arrive at my appointment on time. I wished I had Antonio there with me but I still had to check on my baby even if it meant doing it without him. I was still emotional when I checked in with the receptionist and sat down in the waiting area but I hid it with a fake smile. The nurse called me to the back and took my vitals the same way she had done at my previous appointment. I thought I would be happy to see my doctor when he came in but I suddenly became overly emotional since he looked just like Antonito. I immediately started sobbing.

"What's wrong? Why are you crying?" he asked as he took a seat in front of me.

"It's personal and I don't think it would be professional for me to tell you all the drama I have in my life right now," I claimed as I wiped the tears from my eyes.

"I was expecting to see your significant other as well but I don't think it's unprofessional for us to converse if it makes you feel better. Stress isn't good for the baby or for you so I'm all ears," he said as he handed me some tissue.

"He broke up with me last night. He thinks I betrayed him but I didn't. It just looked as if I did." Although he was basically a stranger, I felt comfortable venting to him. I also didn't have many other people who I could trust venting to at this point.

"Do you want to talk about it Angel? What do you mean it looked as if you did?"

"It's a long story but my father has been trying to break us up ever since we first started dating. He orchestrated the meeting with my best friend and her boyfriend and took photos of her boyfriend and me as if we were a couple. It looked like I was cheating but I wasn't. I was only getting advice on how to tell Antonio that we're expecting because he didn't know yet and I still haven't told him because we ended up having this argument," I managed to say in between my sobbing.

"What type of father deliberately sabotages his daughter's relationship? What's the point of that?" he asked as he handed me another tissue.

"My father is the mayor and he wants to control every aspect of my life including who I date."

"Your father is the mayor of this state?"

"Yeah, I'm sure you've seen him in the media because that's where he lives," I spat.

"Wow, I hope everything gets better for you and Antonio but for now I need you to be healthy and as stress-free as possible. You've lost a few pounds since your last visit and your blood pressure is high. I would hate to put you on bed rest so soon so please take of yourself."

"Thank you, I appreciate you for listening. I really needed that."

"I'm here anytime you need me and now that you're calmer, let's hear the heartbeat of the baby."

Chapter Nineteen:

Kenneth

"You won't believe what happened today?" I said to Greg.

"Did things go well with Antonio?"

"That's what I wanted to talk to you about. I was expecting Antonio to be at the appointment today but he wasn't there because apparently they broke up last night. Check this out though, guess who Angel's father is?" I asked.

"I have no idea so just tell me."

"The mayor, Greg. The mayor is her father. Do you see where I'm going with this? Are you putting two and two together like I am? What happened when you had that meeting with him?"

"Yeah, I definitely see where you're going with this. Now that you mention it, he was hell bent on me focusing on other suspects. I could tell he was referring to Antonio and his brothers but he never explicitly mentioned them. He just allured to there being more than one perpetrator. Explain what's going on with Angel and Antonio."

"Long story short, he sabotaged their relationship. He used some photos to manipulate Antonio into thinking Angel was cheating on him but most importantly, I think his next step is to harm my son. How do you suggest I handle this?"

"Let me brainstorm for a minute before you make any sudden moves. I still need to locate Von Harris so give me a day or two to pull some strings."

"I'll give you that but in the meantime I need to get in touch with Antonio before he makes the biggest mistake of his life. I can see history repeating itself in this relationship like Angela and I and I need to put a stop to it before things get any worse."

"That's fine. Just make sure you do that and only that for now."

"Okay, I hear you." *I wasn't making any promises though.*

."

Chapter Twenty:

Antonio

I laid on top of the sheets with my hands behind my head as I thought about everything that had occurred in my life thus far. I thought about being molested by Rachel during my childhood and how it affected me to today. I thought about my falling out with Byron and most importantly, I thought about Angel. Although I was heartbroken by her actions, I still loved her and hadn't stopped thinking about her. I missed her touch. She was the only woman to ever understand me. I didn't always need to explain my emotions to her because she was so good at reading my body language and she even accurately guessed my thoughts. I'd been crying ever since I saw those photos and I honestly would've never guessed that I'd be so devastated with her cheating. I didn't realize that I was so in love with Angel that I'd be here crying like a big ass baby. I was far from the man I was when I first met her. I could admit that her presence softened my tough exterior, or better yet my defense mechanism. Surprisingly, she had managed to tear down my walls of protection that I had built so long ago. My phone started ringing and suddenly brought me out of my trance. When I looked at the screen, I realized that it was Angel calling me again. I was tempted to answer just so I could hear her voice because I missed it but my pride and ego decided that it was too soon to speak to her. I needed space to reflect on my life. As soon as my phone stopped ringing I went right back into the mental cocoon that I'd locked myself in since I saw the photos and the file. My phone rang again but this time it was Tevin.

"What's good bro. Did you find anything else?" I asked as I sat up in the bed and tried to hide the fact that I had been crying.

"Yeah and what I found is more bizarre than before. This shit is getting kind of hectic to be honest with you."

"Elaborate."

"The IP address associated with the device that was used to steal our log in information linked back to a computer desktop but the location is what's fucking weird. The desktop is located at the 3ʳᵈ district police station. That's Julian's district." I couldn't believe what I was hearing.

"What the fuck?!?! So you mean to tell me that someone who works for the police department is responsible for stealing our money?"

"Yes, that's exactly what I'm saying. IP addresses don't lie. I have the ability to pinpoint the exact computer but I need to be within a close radius so we gone have to make a trip down to the station."

"Fuck! I never wanted attention from the police and now you're telling me that I'd have to voluntarily walk in there while I'm being investigated? Fuck!" I yelled.

"Either that or I can have Julian come with me but I'm the only one who knows how to pinpoint the computer so I need someone else to be a distraction. I just need five minutes max."

"Call Julian and tell him what's going on to see if he can go with you. Julian being inside of the police department would be more ideal anyways for obvious reasons. It wouldn't be smart for me to go inside with you but I can definitely take y'all down there to make sure everything goes as planned. Where are you now?"

"I'm at my office right now. Why?"

"I'm about to come get you. When you call Julian tell him to meet us at the police station as soon as possible."

"Alright, I got you."

I grabbed my wallet and car keys and rushed out the front door. I buckled my seatbelt and sped off to grab Tev because I was too anxious to know what the fuck was really going on. I was listening to the radio as I drove when I heard the song "They Don't Know" by Jon B began to play which instantly reminded of Angel. "Of course a song reminding me of her would play when I was trying my hardest to forget about her," I thought to myself. It was as if the lyrics were specifically about us and our relationship. I damn near broke down all over again by the end of the song when he said "You're my angel, nothing is gonna make you fall from heaven." I quickly changed the radio station in hopes of finding a hip-hop station when I was met with yet another song that reminded me of her. The song from our first date "I Want to Be Your Man" was playing when I stopped at a red light. I decided to just turn off the radio and ride in silence. All of these reminders were making me more emotional than I cared to be.

I scooped up Tevin before making my way down to the police station. My heart was racing because I didn't know what would come out of this attempt to find more information about our missing money. I just knew that this was a risky move considering how we were technically corporate criminals but I'd be damned if we didn't at least try to get our money back. Julian was already here so all Tevin needed to do was follow him inside since this was his stomping grounds. Tev pulled out some high-tech hand-held device before getting out of the truck. I told him good luck and watched him make his way inside the building. I was sweating bullets as I waited to hear back from them since it had now passed five minutes max that Tevin claimed he needed. I checked my watch after a few more minutes before seeing Julian and Tevin calmly walk back out to my truck. When they approached me Julian spoke first.

"Bro, I need you to come inside of the station. You're going to want to hear this for yourself."

"What is it nigga? You know I hate being blindsided."

"It's a long story but I need you to come meet someone. He can shed some light on what's going on."

"You sure I'm good to go in there? From my understanding they've been investigating me." I was clearly paranoid. I'll be damned if I go to prison.

"Come on bro, we wouldn't lead you into a trap. Trust me when I say Von isn't the only one who has connections and protection. Just follow me," said Julian.

I turned off my car and followed my brothers inside the station. Although they assured me that everything was cool, I was still nervous as hell. Walking past all of the cops and detectives made me feel uneasy. Julian finally approached an office and opened the door. When I walked inside, an older black dude stood up from the desk and reached out to shake my hand. He looked familiar but I couldn't recall where I recognized his face from.

"No need to be alarmed Antonio. My name is Detective Greg. How are you doing?"

"I'll be better once I find out what all this is about so I'm listening." I said as I shook his hand and took a seat.

"I'll get straight to the point. Thanks to Tevin, I finally have the opportunity to let you know why the money is missing from y'all savings account. The story is deeper than what you think and it's really not my place to tell you guys everything at the moment. For one, this isn't the place to have this conversation and secondly, I took the money for someone who also wants to protect you. If you guys can meet me at the café shop on Center Street in thirty minutes, we can all sit down to answer any of the questions you may have." When I looked at him I could tell he was being honest and I knew he respected me since he looked me in the eyes when he spoke to me. Now I was more curious than ever to hear this brother out.

"Alright, we'll see you in thirty minutes. Let's roll y'all," I announced as I stood and left. I waited until we were all seated in my truck before asking my brothers a couple of questions myself. I wanted clarity on how we even got to this point.

"So what happened in the station?"

"So once we got inside the station, my device pinpointed the office with the desktop. However, before we could even confirm the computer, Julian informed me that the office belonged to the detective he'd been collaborating with to put away Von. Since Julian was already working with Detective Greg, it was easy to get him to step away from his office. Julian told him he wanted to show him something in the evidence room which gave me all the time I needed to confirm that this was definitely the desktop used to steal our money. Once they returned to the office, we questioned Detective Greg and this is where we are now," said Tevin.

"Interesting. Well, we're about to get down to the bottom of this once and for all."

We waited inside the café casually conversing until Greg and his unknown party finally arrived. I observed both men as they made their way to our table. The guy with Detective Greg looked awfully familiar to me as well. He was dark skinned, tall and had a head full of grey hair. He had on sunglasses which I thought was weird considering he was no longer outside. Greg took a seat and then his friend followed suit. I wanted to get straight to the point but first I needed to see this dude's eyes.

"I'm Tony. I didn't catch your name," I said as I reached over to shake his hand.

"I'm Kenneth."

"Do you mind taking your shades off?" He seemed to hesitate before slowly removing them, folding the arms and placing them on the table. He kept his head tilted slightly which made me even more curious of him.

"I would like to start by saying that you all may not know a lot about us but we know exactly who you are. We've been looking after you guys since y'all were bad ass little boys playing ball in the park. I'm certain the question now is who the hell are we and why have we been looking after y'all? I'll let my best friend Kenny explain that and then we'll discuss the money thing," said Greg. I looked at Kenny who finally held his head up allowing me to get a good look at him and I'll be damned! It was like looking in a mirror! *What the fuck is really going on here*?

"I'd been planning an extravagant speech for this very moment when I was finally able to sit down and have a man to man conversation but what it all simply boils down to is that I am your biological father Antonio. It's a long story and if you're willing to hear me out, I'll be more than happy to tell you anything you want to know." *What did he just say to me?*

"Is this some kind of fucking joke?" I didn't know why I instantly became angry.

"No, I'm serious. You can look at me and tell that I'm serious," said Kenneth.

"So you mean to tell me that you've been lurking in the shadows ever since I was a kid and didn't do shit about raising me? What type of fucking man are you?" I thought about all of the abuse I endured in my childhood. He could have been there to stop it yet he left me to fend for myself.

"It's deeper than what you know Antonio. Everything isn't black and white. I wanted to tell you. I wanted to be the man you needed me to be but I wasn't in the mental space to be that for you. Can we talk somewhere in private?" he pleaded.

"Nah fuck that! I think I've heard enough from you," I announced as I stood up and left. When I reached my truck, he was right behind me. I opened the driver's door but he stopped me dead in my tracks and slammed it shut before I could get inside.

"So you gone run away just like that? Is that how you handle all of your problems?" he asked as we stood face to face.

"Nah, unlike you I don't run away from responsibility. I take care of my obligations like a fucking man is supposed to! I would never leave my seed to fend for themselves!" I yelled as I pushed him out of my face.

"See you talking like you know every fucking thing! What if yo ass got a seed out here and you don't even know it! When is the last time you talked to Angel?" he yelled as he pushed my back against the truck. I was gonna swing on him but him bringing up Angel's name stopped me midair.

"How do you know about her?" I asked as I started to calm down.

"I told you it's a long story. Hop in my truck and take a ride with me. I have something to show you." I was hesitant but I was also curious to hear what he had to say after mentioning Angel so I obliged. At first, it was awkward because we were both quiet. Then, he finally broke the silence.

"Look, this isn't easy for me either and if you don't want to speak then fine just hear me out. I'll start with Angel first. I met her not too long ago but it was really serendipity. Not sure if you know this but I'm a medical doctor and she just so happens to be a patient at the hospital where I practice. It wasn't up until a few weeks ago when she actually became one of my patients."

"What was the reason for her visit?" I asked.

"With doctor-patient confidentiality, this really isn't my place to tell you but considering everything that has transpired I'll go ahead and speak against my better judgment. She came to me to confirm whether or not she was pregnant. The pregnancy test came back positive. It was then that she described the lucky guy and when she said your name and described your features, I knew you were the father."

"Well it's over between us and that probably ain't even my baby."

"See this is why I had to reach out to you because you're making the biggest mistake of your life right now. Do you know who her father is?"

"Yeah, I already know this. He's the mayor," I said arrogantly.

"Okay smart ass, did you know that the mayor is working with Von Harris? He's been protecting him and wants you to take the fall as the city's King Pin. Did you know that he arranged that meeting with Angel and her so called best friend to frame her and make it look like she was cheating on you? She was all worked up and distraught at her last visit because of it. She's losing weight and her blood pressure was higher than normal for a pregnant woman. You claim to take care of your responsibilities. Well Angel and the baby are now a part of your responsibilities." It all hit me at once and then everything started falling into place. She didn't really have food poisoning. She had morning sickness and the night I confronted her about the pictures she was probably trying to tell me that she was pregnant. It suddenly dawned on me that her "best friend" could have easily planted that shit in her bedroom. I felt like the biggest asshole on the planet. I had to get my baby back.

"What else do you know?"

"I know that you love her and she loves you. Don't make the same mistake I made with you and your mother. Trust me, you'll regret it for the rest of your life." He claimed as he pulled into a cemetery.

"What mistake?" I asked as I followed his lead stepping out of the truck. He walked up to a tombstone and stopped.

"Your mother was and always will be the most beautiful woman I've ever met. No other woman could ever fill her shoes. She was highly intelligent, beautiful and nurturing. She was everything a man could ever ask for in a woman. My father was something like Angel's father; a controlling narcissist if there ever was one. He didn't want me to date Angela, your mother, because she was poor and was the daughter of a single mother but I fell in love with her. I found out we were expecting you while I was still in medical school. When my father found out, he wanted to abort you and even gave me the money to do so but instead I used the money to set up an apartment for your mother and me. After giving birth to you she started changing and I wasn't there to help her or take care of you. I was too busy building a life for us financially that I neglected my responsibilities. While I was in school, Greg called and told that me she killed herself and put you up for adoption. I didn't handle the grieving process very well. I still struggle with what happened and felt responsible for her death and losing you. I looked for you for years and when I found you, you were thirteen. I can admit that I took the cowardly way out but I'm here now." He pulled out his wallet and handed me a photo of my mother. He was right when he said she was beautiful. I tried to hold back my tears but I started crying a river.

"Don't make the same mistakes I did son," he repeated as he hugged me. He patted my back and for the first time I bonded with someone who was actually a part of my bloodline. I finally felt like I belonged. He explained to me how and why the money was taken from our account as we headed back to the café. At this point, I didn't really care about the money. The only thing on my mind now was visiting Angel. I hoped and prayed that she would forgive me.

Chapter Twenty-One:

Von

Although I had protection from the police thanks to the mayor, I still didn't trust his ass because he was the type of dude who was only concerned about himself. Once he was done using you, you'd be discarded as if you never even existed. I was already well aware of this so I took every precaution I could to protect my damn self. I recorded every phone call and every interaction just to have an insurance policy on his ass. You never knew exactly who to trust in a game like this and even though he and I had been working together for years, you never really knew what someone was capable of when their back was against the wall.

Even though I despised Antonio's ass, I had to admit that deep down I had respect for him. He made thousands of dollars selling drugs and had yet to be caught. Somehow he managed to stay ten steps ahead of everyone else. Whatever you thought you knew about his drug cartel, I was pretty sure he had already thoroughly thought out every possible consequence. The risk versus the reward had already been determined so pinpointing a loophole in his drug operations was like trying to find a needle in a hay stack. He was so low key about everything that I still didn't even know who his supplier was. I had eyes and ears on every corner yet no one saw or heard shit when it came to how he handled business. The walls were closing in and my deadline was quickly approaching. My hired help still hadn't been able to get me any closer to Summer so my plan involving her to get money from their account turned out to be a dead end. The money the mayor fronted me was damn near gone so I needed to make something happen soon. Lord only knew what would happen to me if I didn't give him anything leading to Antonio's arrest. If he wasn't re-elected, he'd surely take that bullshit out on me. I went inside the liquor store and grabbed a bottle of Hennessey because the weed wasn't cutting it anymore. I needed something stronger to shake these nerves. As I sipped from the bottle, my burner phone rang. I knew it was the devil himself calling to collect. The liquor burned my throat and chest and I quickly swallowed and answered the phone.

"Your time is almost up. Do you have anything for me?"

"Yeah, I got something for you. I need to meet with you in person to discuss it though. I don't do business over the phone."

"Okay, well bring your ass back to the city and come see me."

"It's not that simple. I need some funds to make the drive back. Trust me, the info I have will be worth every penny," I lied.

"You always need something don't you? How much do you need this time?" he spat.

"Just a couple hundred for gas, food and hotel stay when I stop to rest. This drive isn't a fucking walk in the park. You got me out here in the middle of no man's land."

"Listen, I have a charity event coming up on Saturday to fund my campaign. It's going to be a lot of people there giving away money so if this information is really as concrete as you say it is then you can expect a nice chunk of money right then and there. That's almost a week from now so I expect you to make it in time. This is an upscale event which means no thug attire. Don't disappoint me," he announced before hanging up.

The truth was the only thing I had on Antonio was the warehouse where he moved his product but I had never actually stepped foot inside. However, Summer did tell me that it was locked up like fucking Fort Knox. Only the brothers had access to it and at this point, I didn't give a fuck how the mayor planned on using this information. That was his problem. I stopped at a gas station and filled my tank before hopping on the freeway to head back to the city. My heart raced as I sped down the freeway leading back to the bullshit I had left some weeks ago. The goal was to get the money from the mayor and then get the fuck back out of dodge for good.

I had finally made it after driving almost three days straight with just a few naps in between here and there. I didn't even use a hotel, I just slept in my car and pocketed the rest of the money. When I made it back to the city, the first thing I did was shower at one of my lil chick's crib since I had lost my properties due to foreclosure. I only had one day to prepare for this event which meant that I needed to find some business attire to wear. I headed to *Men's Warehouse* to get fitted for a suit to wear tomorrow evening. I decided on an all-black suit with a matching belt and dress shoes. I was in desperate need for a haircut since I'd been on the run but I didn't want to risk being seen in a barbershop so I called my barber and asked him to pay me a visit at my girl's crib so he could cut my hair at her house. It cost me extra but it was worth every penny. I felt like a new man after he got me right. Once he left, I chilled in my truck and rolled a blunt. I thought about Summer and my grandsons as I sat in silence. For some reason, I felt like my time on this planet was soon coming to an end. I looked at myself in the rearview mirror and accepted my fate. With all the dirt I'd done in my lifetime, I was surprised to feel at peace for once. Although I had a strained relationship with Summer, I felt guided to pay her a visit so I decided to make my way over to her house. I walked up the stairs and knocked on the front door. After a few moments, Byron answered.

"What the fuck are you doing here?" he snapped.

"I don't want any trouble. I just want to speak with Summer. I got something for her," I claimed.

"Wait here," he demanded before closing the door. I hadn't been welcome in their home for quite some time and I could understand why. A few moments passed before Summer came to the door. She stepped outside pulling the door shut behind her.

"What do you want daddy?" she asked as she folded her arms across her chest.

"I want to give you something to keep if something were to ever happen to me. I want you to have this for safe-keeping," I claimed as I handed her a black safety deposit box.

"What is this?" she asked as she accepted the box.

"Don't worry about what it is right now but if something happens to me then I want you to open this box and you'll understand why." I took the key to the lock box off my key ring and handed it to her.

"Is someone after you? Should I be worried?"

"Don't worry about me Summer. I know we don't always get along but just know that people can change. I love you and I love my grandsons. I'll see you soon," I stated as I made my way back to the truck. I had a gut feeling that this would be my last time seeing her.

Chapter Twenty-Two

Antonio

After I left the café, I dropped Tevin back off at his office and then headed to the mall. I had already made up my mind that Angel was definitely the one for me before any of this bullshit ever happened. I had even planned on going ring shopping so that I could propose to her but of course, all of this drama got in the way of that. I had already knew her ring size from when I swiped one of the rings out of her jewelry box in order to find out. When I made it to the mall, I went straight to *Zales* so I could buy a ring. I was confused about which one to get so I was glad when the store attendant approached me.

"Can I help you sir?" said the white girl behind the counter.

"Yeah, I'm looking for an engagement ring for my girlfriend."

"Well she's certainly one lucky girl. Do you know what type of cut she would like?"

"I'm not sure. I was hoping you could help me with that."

"If you describe what type of woman she is then I can certainly help."

"She's the type of woman who isn't really materialistic. She prefers to be treated like royalty rather than just dressing like it but somehow she always looks expensive," I chuckled to myself. "She's gentle but feisty when she has to be. She's the most beautiful woman I've ever met but she's really down to earth. She's a poetic contradiction personified," I announced as I thought about how lucky I truly was to have met her.

"Wow, I've never heard any man speak about their significant other in such a way and the sparkle in your eyes as you spoke about her is so touching! I think I have the perfect ring for you!" she screamed as she scurried to the opposite end of the counter. I followed behind her when she finally stopped in front of a section filled with princess cut diamond rings. She handed me a silver ring with a squared princess cut diamond.

"This ring is elegant but it's not too flashy. It's one carat but with a round infinity design which, in my opinion, makes it look extremely romantic. I honestly think she'll fall in love with this ring," she claimed.

"I like it. I'll take it," I claimed as I pulled out my wallet.

"You don't want to know the price?"

"It doesn't matter because I'm buying it regardless. I'll take it in a size 5 ½," I demanded.

"Okay, the man has spoken. I'll have this ready for you momentarily."

After I left the mall I went straight to Angel's house. Her bedroom light was on so I knew she was home. I put the ring in my pocket and rang the doorbell. After waiting for a couple of minutes, I rang the doorbell again and still no answer. I stepped off the porch to see if her bedroom light was still on and it wasn't. I'd be damned if I gave up that easily so I went back to my truck to search my phone for the song "I Want to Be Your Man" by Zapp and Roger. I knew she didn't want me to cause a scene in her neighborhood but I blasted the song as loud as it could go through my speakers. I waited with the driver's door open to see if she would react. Her bedroom light suddenly popped back on as she poked her head out the window. She was cute even when she was angry.

"What the hell are you doing here Antonio?" she yelled.

"What does it look like I'm doing? I'm trying to get my woman back!" I yelled back at her. I turned the music down to hear what she had to say.

"Now you want to pop back in my life after you've been ignoring me for weeks? Life doesn't work on your terms Antonio so leave me alone and go back to wherever you were before you met me," she claimed just before slamming the window shut. I knew she would be upset but I didn't think this evening would play out quite like this. I was just about to knock on her door again when my phone rang. It was Julian.

"What's up bro?"

"I just got word from one of my friends that Von is back in town. He was spotted buying a suit from *Men's Warehouse* so I'm assuming he'll be attending the mayor's event tomorrow. You down to go?"

"Yeah you already know I'm down. I think we all should pay a visit to Byron before the event tomorrow. This drama between us has been going on long enough. It's time to nip this shit in the bud."

"Yeah, I agree with you. I'll let everyone else know. I don't know about y'all but I'll be strapped with my gun just in case some shit goes down."

"I'll be prepared just in case. You never know what to expect with Von anyways."

"Alright, I'll see you soon."

"Okay cool."

Even though I didn't want to, I decided to give Angel her space. I'd rather be lying up under her but I understood that she was still pissed off. I went home to get some sleep. I was sure that I'd need all of the rest I could get for tomorrow. When I woke up the next morning, I showered and ate some breakfast. When I finished eating, I went to my closet to find a suit to wear. I called Tevin as I searched my closet and waited for him to answer.

"Hello," said Tevin.

"Yo, have you talked to Julian today?"

"Yeah, he called me earlier and told me that you wanted us to visit B. I think this is long overdue anyway. I miss my nigga," Tevin chuckled.

"Yeah, I'm not gone lie. I miss his crazy ass too. We all we got so I'll be damned if this bullshit comes between us. We all need to be on the same page so it's only right we go see him."

"What time were you planning on going over there?"

"I'm actually getting dressed right now since we're going to the event later. You are going to the event right?" I asked as I picked out an all-black suit. The color black always made me feel like a boss.

"Yeah, you already know I'm not missing this shit. I heard Von was gone be there too so I'd be crazy to miss out on some entertainment. I might have to bring some popcorn for this show," Tevin laughed again.

"Yeah, it's been awhile since we've seen him face to face so I can't wait to see how he reacts to all of us popping up on his ass."

"Aye, can you come scoop me before you head to Byron's house? Wifey is driving my truck and I'll be damned if I drive around the city in a pink Mercedes."

"Yeah, I got you bro. I'll be pulling up in an hour so be ready."

"Okay, cool."

I quickly dressed, brushed my hair and my teeth and then sprayed my favorite cologne. I didn't care where I'm going, I couldn't leave the house without looking good and smelling presentable. I tried calling Angel again as I drove to pick up Tevin but she didn't answer. I had the ring in my pocket because I had a gut feeling that she would actually be present at her father's event. The press would definitely be there so I'm sure he wouldn't have it any other way. When I pulled up to Tevin's house I honked the horn and waited for him to come out. When he finally came outside, I noticed he was wearing a suit that was damn near identical to mine. He hopped in my truck and buckled his seat belt.

"I see everyone wants to be like Tony Montana," I joked with him.

"Nigga, what are you talking about?"

"I'm talking about you damn near wearing the same suit as me," I chuckled.

"Yeah, I always wanted to be like you when I grew up," he said sarcastically.

"Yeah, I already know because I'm a boss."

"You must really be feeling yourself right now?" laughed Tevin.

"Nah I'm just in a really good mood. I mean why wouldn't I be? I'm about to patch some shit up with baby bro, I'm building a bond with my biological father, I'm proposing to my girl soon and I have a little one on the way… shit life is great right now!" I declared.

"You got a baby on the way? Not Mr. I always wear a rubber so bitches don't catch me slipping. What?" he claimed as if he didn't believe me.

"Yeah man, I have a baby on the way and it's with an amazing woman," I claimed as I thought about Angel.

"You already got a ring?" asked Tevin.

"Yeah, you think she'll like it?" I asked as I pulled it out of my pocket and handed it to him while I drove.

"Diamonds are a girl's best friend and she's definitely gone love this one. This shit right here is nice," he claimed as he examined the ring.

"I just hope she forgives me for the dumb shit I've been doing lately."

"You must really love her. I never thought I'd see the day a woman would ever have you proposing or having babies. I'm happy for you bro."

"She's definitely the one for me. Good looking bro."

We continued to chop it up as we headed to Byron's house. He didn't know we were coming over so I told Jasper and Julian to wait until Tevin and I pulled up before knocking on the door. When we got there, Julian and Jasper were already waiting in Jasper's truck. We all got out of our vehicles and gathered before knocking on B's front door.

"Is everybody prepared in case some shit goes down tonight?" I asked as we greeted each other with handshakes and hugs.

"You already know I'm trained to go," announced Julian.

"I'm ready for whatever," claimed Jasper.

"My shit is strapped on my ankle just in case I need it," said Tevin. Despite being in the drug game, we never had to hurt anyone before which didn't mean we weren't prepared to if push came to shove but of course violence was always our last resort. If we ever needed to resort to violence, it just meant we weren't handling business effectively or intelligently.

"Sounds good, I got my shit on me too. Man, y'all look sharp as hell. No more holey jeans and torn soles at the bottom of our shoes huh?" I asked as I reminisced about the old days.

"Hell nah! We're some grown ass successful black men now! Anything is possible when you learn how to turn your pain into power," exclaimed Jasper.

"I'm glad y'all wore y'all watches because we may have a short meeting at the warehouse tonight after the event. I want to cross a few T's before the night is over," I claimed. Everyone lifted their sleeves to show me that they had on their watches to enter the warehouse. We all made our way to Byron's front door and rang the doorbell. After a few moments, Summer opened the door. She was shocked to say the least.

"Wow, what are y'all doing here? Well don't you fellas look nice! I love the suits by the way!" she claimed as she hugged us. She had never been this happy to see us before. I wondered what sparked this change in her behavior.

"Is Byron home?" asked Tevin.

"Yeah, come in and make yourselves at home. I'll grab him for you." We all stood in the living room as we heard Summer and Byron chatting amongst themselves. When he finally appeared in the living room, he had shaving cream on his face and a razor in his hand. He was shocked to see us too.

"What's good bro. How you been doing," I asked to break the ice.

"I'm good. I'm just shocked to see all of y'all here. Why is everyone so dressed up?"

"We're attending an event tonight but first we wanted to stop and chop it up with you. I also wanted to apologize for the shit I said. I shouldn't have disrespected you or Summer in that way and for that I apologize. Are we good?" I asked as I waited with my hands in my pockets for his response. He had on his poker face so I couldn't read him.

"Come on, y'all should know we gone always be good. We go through shit but we get through shit too. Brothers from unknown mothers is a bond that will never be broken," he claimed as he hugged me and the rest of the brothers.

"Man, I missed yo ass," laughed Jasper.

"Man, I missed y'all too. I feel like I just got out of jail and shit! I was mad bored without y'all," laughed Byron.

"Cool, now that we're all on the same page again we have to head out because this event is starting soon," I announced.

"Alright, let me finish shaving and getting dressed. I'll be ready in 20."

"Bring yo heat too. You might need it for tonight and don't forget yo watch." I reminded him as we left to wait outside.

"Shit, say no more," said Byron. I was happy to see my bro again. I hadn't talked to him in weeks.

Bryon rode with me and Tevin as we made our way to the event. I was nervous and didn't know what to expect. My pops called me and told me that he and Greg would also be in attendance just to watch over things. I must admit that I was glad that my father would be present. It made life seem more normal. When we made it to the venue, valet parked our cars as we gathered out front. We all had on our sunglasses as we strutted inside the building side by side, swag on point. The charity event was in full effect and already almost packed to capacity. My eyes immediately searched the crowd for Angel's face but instead I spotted my pops and Greg at the bar so I approached them.

"What's up pops?" I asked as I hugged him. It felt good to call him that.

"Nothing much. I was just having a good drink with a good friend. Have you checked on Angel?"

"Yeah, I tried but she doesn't want anything to do with me right now."

"Just give her some space for now. She'll come around when she's ready. She reminds me a lot of your mother. She was gentle but also stubborn as hell," laughed pops.

"Yeah, that's probably where I get it from. I want to show you something," I announced as I took the ring out of my pocket and handed it to him.

"This ring is nice. I'm sure she's going to love it too. I'm proud of you for stepping up and being a man. That's all I ever wanted for my son."

"I thought about what you said at the cemetery and you were right. I don't want to look back on my life and regret not stepping into my manhood so for that, I thank you."

"No need to thank me Antonio. It's my job to teach you the tough lessons I've already learned through experience. I only want what's best for you."

"Well I appreciate it. How did y'all know about this event anyway?" I asked Greg.

"I know people in high and low places. It's kind of my job to know these things," laughed Greg. "No but seriously a little birdy told me to make it my business to attend this event. I always follow up on tips and leads. That's how I solve all of my cases."

I continued to converse with them until I noticed Angel walking inside the event. It was as if everything and everyone disappeared whenever I seen her. She must've been doing magic on me because I saw no one but her. I excused myself from the conversation and followed her trail. The closer I got the more nervous I became. I was a few feet behind her as she stood with her back towards me. She wore a black strapless gown that was fitted at the top and flowing at the bottom. She had her hair in a sleek bun which happened to be my favorite hairstyle and as I approached her I could smell the scent of her perfume. When I finally mustered up the courage I tapped her on her shoulder. I was still nervous because I didn't know how she'd react.

"What are you doing here? Are you stalking me now?" she snapped.

"I don't have to stalk you Angel. I'm here to take care of some business," I announced as I scanned her from head to toe. Her hips and breast were fuller since the last time I'd seen her and I couldn't stop myself from staring at her. She was glowing and I was mesmerized for sure.

"You're always handling business Antonio. That's nothing new. That seems to be the only thing you care about," she claimed as she tried to walk away from me before I gently grabbed her by the arm.

"You and I both know that's not true. I care about you. I love you. I cherish the ground you walk on and if you said jump, I'd ask you how high and how many times. That's how much I love you Angel. It's very seldom that you're blessed to find your equal so I'll be damned if I just let you walk out of my life," I claimed as I stepped closer to her. "I love you and I love our unborn child," I stated as I rubbed her stomach.

"How do you know that I'm pregnant?" she asked. I could tell she was emotional as tears formed in her eyes.

"A little birdy told me that you're pregnant. Actually, the little birdy is over there at the bar," I claimed as I waved at my dad who waved back in return. "That's my biological father who I just found out about. It's a long story that I'd like to share with you later," I stated as I held her hand.

"Wow, well that explains why he reminded me of you so much," she finally smiled at me.

"Can you please forgive me for the way I've treated you? I want to step up and be the man you deserve," I continued.

"If you want to be the man I deserve then you'll have to prove it to me. Otherwise, don't waste my time Antonio," she announced as she tried to walk away again. I pulled the ring out of my pocket and dropped down to one knee. She looked at me with tears in her eyes and one hand covering her mouth. By this time, we were drawing attention from people at the event but I didn't care. I had tunnel vision only for her.

"Is this proof enough for you Angel? I'm right here, right now on one knee in front of everyone because I am the man you deserve and I want you and only you. Will you marry me?" I pronounced as I waited anxiously for her answer. She couldn't verbally respond because she was sobbing at this point. She sat on my bended knee and hugged me.

"Is that a yes?" I asked her. She nodded her head up and down as she continued to cry. I placed the ring on her finger and kissed her. Lord only knew just how much I missed this. My brothers and everyone else cheered us on as we embraced one another. However, there was one person in the crowd that didn't seem too happy. After the crowd settled down, I walked across the room to have a conversation with her father. I could tell by the look on his face that this wouldn't be a friendly conversation.

"You won't be celebrating for long so enjoy your fifteen minutes of fame while it lasts," he claimed as I approached him.

"I noticed that you like to pull strings behind the scenes but where I'm from, we bring that shit to your front door. I don't give a fuck who you are. You don't want these problems," I declared as I faced him man to man sizing him up.

"That's so typical of a thug to threaten someone. I hope you can keep up that thug routine behind bars too," he boasted.

"I don't make threats mayor, I make promises. You think you got it all figured out huh? Just know that in this chess game we call life, you can never beat me," I announced as I walked away to join my soon to be wife and family. When I made it back to my circle, I assured Angel that everything was okay between her father and me even though that wasn't true. I just didn't want to stress her out while she was carrying my child.

As we continued to talk I noticed that Von finally decided to join the party. I had never seen this nigga wear a suit before but I must admit that he was casket sharp. He looked as if he was in a hurry when he approached the mayor and whispered in his ear. They immediately disappeared into the crowd shortly thereafter. Byron wanted to follow them but I stopped him in his tracks. This wasn't the time or the place to start an altercation. There were way too many people around for that. I wasn't worried about what would transpire between the two of them because little did they know I planned for shit like this. Von was leaving just as quickly as he arrived only this time he was carrying a black suitcase as he rushed for the exit. I decided to let him walk away scot-free despite my brothers wanting to confront him. They didn't see the bigger picture the way I did. Although Von was working with the mayor, the mayor was going to silence him for good. This I knew for a fact. After Greg gave me the run down on the history between the mayor and Von, I realized that Von had gathered so much dirt on the mayor over the years that he was now more of a liability than an asset. I asked myself, "Why would the mayor let Von leave the city alive when he ultimately had the power to destroy his image, his career and he even had the power to blackmail him and put the mayor behind bars for good?" I was positive that Von would be smart enough to know that his days to live were numbered.

Shortly after Von left the venue, there was a huge explosion that nearly shook the entire building. People frantically scurried outside to find out the commotion. When my brothers and I made it outside, Von's truck was engulfed in flames. I knew he was inside of the truck and I also knew that the mayor was behind this hit. I was just surprised that the nigga was bold enough to do the shit at his own charity event. Of course it was risky but it was also a smart move since he already had an alibi.

Greg immediately called for backup and the venue was surrounded by the fire department and police department within minutes. As firefighters put out the flames from the explosion, police officers started canvasing the crowd for any witnesses. Greg approached the chief of police when he arrived on scene. Shortly after they started conversing, the mayor approached and interrupted their conversation. I could tell that Greg and the mayor were arguing but I didn't know why. The mayor glanced over at me with a devilish grin on his face as he walked away. As soon as he was out of sight, police surrounded my brothers and me forcing us into handcuffs. I kissed Angel just before they shoved us into separate police cars. I was beyond pissed. When we made it to the police station they put each of us in separate interrogation rooms. I was fuming as I waited for someone to question me. It felt like forever before this tall, white, bald dude dressed in a black polo shirt and black dress pants finally entered the room. He looked me in the eyes as he took a seat across from me.

"Do you know why you're here Antonio?"

"No but I'm sure you're going to tell me anyway."

"We have reason to believe that you're involved in the murder of Von Harris."

"Really? What would make you believe that detective?"

"Well, the fact that your old "business partner" who is conveniently now your enemy ends up blown to a million pieces while you are in the same vicinity is what make me believe that."

"There were tons of other people in the same vicinity as well so what does that prove?"

"Yeah but you and your brothers were the only ones armed with weapons. Care to explain that?"

"So now it's illegal for us to exercise our 2nd amendment rights? If you do your job and check our weapons, you'll see that they're all registered and perfectly legal," I fired back at him.

"We also have evidence of drug trafficking at your warehouse. It's only a matter of time before we obtain a search warrant and seize the drugs."

"What drugs? I don't traffic drugs detective. I do however have a string of legitimate businesses but you already know that."

"Right, we'll see what your brothers have to say about you being the master mind behind this whole operation. Don't be surprised if you're the only one left in custody while they go home."

"Okay, good luck with that detective."

"You're the one who needs luck Antonio, not me."

Little did he know that this act didn't worry me one bit. I already had Tevin delete the camera footage at the warehouse and swap out the shipment of drugs with plumbing tools and parts from Jasper's company in order to support our story. I had put this plan into motion the moment I started noticing unmarked cars lurking around the warehouse. I was certain that my employees would only speak highly of me because they were all paid well, treated well and had nothing to do with the drugs. All they knew was that they shipped packages. They didn't know what was inside of them. I sat in the interrogation room for hours before anyone returned. I wasn't even offered a phone call. When the detective finally came back, he picked me up out of my chair and placed me in handcuffs once again.

"Where the fuck are you taking me? I didn't do shit!" I yelled as he pushed me out of the interrogation room.

"I'm taking you to a holding cell. I thought you of all people would know that we can hold you up to 24 hours before releasing you or bringing you up on charges." I saw my brothers getting ready to leave as he continued pushing me into the holding cell. They must have thought I was really dumb enough to fall for this game they were trying to play with me.

"Aye, don't worry bro! We gone have you out of this bitch by the morning!" yelled Byron as I was tossed into the cell. I was in a small ass cell with three other black dudes who were clearly mentally unstable. I guess this was their scare tactic to try and mentally break me down. I sat on the metal bench and forced myself to keep my eyes open. I would be a fool to fall asleep around these niggas. By the morning, I was exhausted, hungry and dehydrated. A police officer finally came and snatched me out of the holding cell only to place me right back into the same interrogation room with the same detective.

"Good morning Antonio. I had such a good night's rest. How about yourself? Those metal cots aren't as comfortable as your pillow top bed huh? Don't worry about that though, you'll get used to the metal eventually." Suddenly, Greg stormed into the room and interrupted the interrogation.

"What the hell are you doing here Greg? This case is out of your jurisdiction!" he yelled as he stood from his chair.

"Some evidence just came across my desk that requires your immediate attention. It should also exonerate Antonio as a suspect as well." I was happy as hell to hear that and I sure was glad Greg had my back once again.

"Show me this so called evidence and I'll be the judge of that," said the detective. I waited alone in the room for about 20 minutes or so before anyone returned. When the detective did come back, he didn't say a single word to me. He just unlocked my handcuffs and motioned for me to leave. Byron and Greg were waiting for me at the front door while I checked out.

"So what evidence came to your desk if you don't mind me asking?" I turned my attention to Greg.

"Von stopped by our house the day before the event and gave Summer a safety deposit box. He must have known that the mayor was scheming against him so he brought a shit load of evidence to

Summer and told her to use it if something were to happen to him. Although he didn't like you, he respected you enough to help you out in the end. I guess you could say he had a sudden change of heart," said Byron.

"The mayor is already being indicted for a long list of charges. I'm sure he won't be happy about being locked up with the criminals he so gladly bragged about putting away," said Greg.

"Where's Angel?" I asked as we exited the double doors of the building. I noticed she was leaning against my Range Rover truck with the keys twirling around her index finger. I ran up to her and picked her up as she cradled her legs around my waist.

"I missed you," I claimed as I kissed her.

"I missed you too," replied Angel. My brothers and my dad hopped out of Tevin's truck and gathered around me, Greg, Byron and Angel.

"So I just have one last question for you Greg."

"What's that?" he answered.

"Where's the money y'all took?"

"We placed it in an offshore account overseas where no one could fuck with it. As a matter of fact, how about we all take a trip to Paris? I sure could use a vacation now that I'm officially retired," he grinned.

"You want to go to Paris baby?" I asked Angel.

"I'll go anywhere you go baby. If you lead, I'll gladly follow."

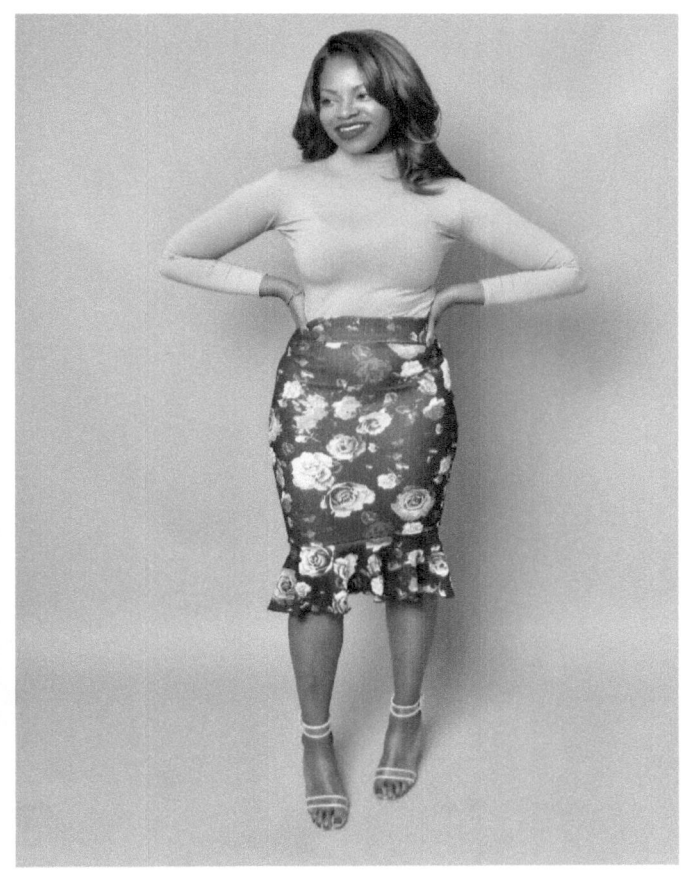

Author T.S. Connor is a poet, self-published author, spoken word artist and most importantly a mother. She believes in no limitations and wishes to inspire those with her words both spoken and written. She encourages people to live life limitless and pursue their dreams by stepping outside the box. May you also be inspired by her words.

Connect with T.S Connor via Facebook by her personal Facebook page at Taniqua Connor or chat with her via AuthorTSConnor.com!

www.ingramcontent.com/pod-product-compliance
Lightning Source LLC
Chambersburg PA
CBHW030530020726
47494CB00004B/1303